# DEATH of a
# SCRIPTWRITER

## The Hamish Macbeth series

# DEATH of a SCRIPTWRITER

## A Hamish Macbeth Murder Mystery

# M. C. BEATON

ROBINSON
London

Constable & Robinson Ltd
3 The Lanchesters
162 Fulham Palace Road
London W6 9ER
www.constablerobinson.com

First published in the USA by Grand Central Publishing,
a division of Hachette Book Group USA, Inc.

This edition published by Robinson,
an imprint of Constable & Robinson, 2009

A copy of the British Library Cataloguing in
Publication data is available from the British Library

UK ISBN: 978-1-84529-909-5

Printed in Great Britain by Clays Ltd, St Ives plc

3 5 7 9 10 8 6 4

For Mary Devery of Cheltenham
With love.

# Hamish Macbeth fans share their reviews . . .

'Treat yourself to an adventure in the Highlands; remember your coffee and scones – for you'll want to stay a while!'

'I do believe I am in love with Hamish.'

'M. C. Beaton's stories are absolutely excellent . . . Hamish is a pure delight!'

'A highly entertaining read that will have me hunting out the others in the series.'

'A new Hamish Macbeth novel is always a treat.'

'Once I read the first mystery I was hooked . . . I love her characters.'

Share your own reviews and comments at
www.constablerobinson.com

# Chapter One

*Alas, that Spring should vanish with the Rose!*
*That Youth's sweet-scented Manuscript should*
*close!*

– Edward Fitzgerald

Patricia Martyn-Broyd had not written a detective story in years.

In her early seventies she had retired to the Highlands of Sutherland on the east side of the village of Cnothan, to a trim, low, white-washed croft house. She had now been living in the outskirts of Cnothan for five years. She had hoped that the wild isolation of her surroundings would inspire her to write again, but every time she sat down in front of her battered old Remington typewriter, she would feel a great weight of failure settling on her shoulders and the words would not come. For the past fifteen years her books had been out of print. Yet her last detective story, published in 1965, *The Case of the Rising Tides*, featuring

1

her Scottish aristocrat detective, Lady Harriet Vere, had been a modest success.

Patricia looked remarkable for her age. She had a head of plentiful snow-white hair, a thin, muscular, upright figure and square 'hunting' shoulders. Her nose was thin and curved like a beak, her pale blue eyes hooded by heavy lids. She was the daughter of a land agent, dead many years now, as was her mother. Patricia had been head girl in her youth at a school more famed for the titles of its pupils than for educational standards. A crush on her English teacher had introduced her to reading detective stories, and then, after an unsuccessful spell on the London scene as a debutante, she had decided to write.

She had never forgotten the thrill of having her first book published. Her plots were complicated and thoroughly researched. She was fond of plots involving railway timetables, the times of high and low tides and London bus routes. Her main character, Lady Harriet Vere, had grown up, as Patricia herself had grown up, in a world where everyone knew their place in society and what was due to their betters. Light relief was provided by a cast of humorous servants or sinister butlers and gardeners and clod-hopping policemen who were always left open-mouthed by the expertise of Lady Harriet.

But as the world changed, Patricia stayed the same, as did her characters. Sales of her books dwindled. She had a private income from a family trust and did not need to find other work. She had at last persuaded herself that a move to the far north of Scotland would inspire her. Although her character, Lady Harriet, was Scottish, Patricia had never been to Scotland before her move north. There was a stubborn streak in Patricia which would not let her admit to herself that she had made a terrible mistake and added the burden of loneliness to the burden of failure.

She had recently returned from a holiday in Athens. The weather in Greece had been bright and sunny and, in the evenings, the streets of Athens were well lit and bustling with people. But all too soon it was back to London, to catch the plane to Inverness. The plane had descended through banks of cloud into Heathrow. How dark and dismal everything had seemed. How cold and rainy. How grim and sour the people. Then the flight to Inverness and down into more rain and darkness, and then the long drive home.

The county of Sutherland is the largest, most under populated area in western Europe, with its lochs and mountains and vast expanses of bleak moorland. As she had unlocked the door of her cottage, the wind had been howling around the low building with a mad, keening sound. A brief thought of suicide flicked through Patricia's weary brain, to be quickly dismissed. Such as the Martyn-Broyds did not commit suicide.

Patricia attended the local Church of Scotland, although she was an Anglican, for the nearest Episcopal church involved too long and weary a drive. She could have made friends, but the ones she considered of her own caste did not want to know her, and the ones who did, she considered beneath her. She was not particularly cold or snobbish, and she was lonely, but it was the way she had been brought up. She did have acquaintances in the village, the local people she stopped to chat to, but no close friends at all.

A week after her return from Athens, she still felt restless and so decided to treat herself to dinner at the Tommel Castle Hotel. The hotel had been the home of Colonel Halburton-Smythe, who had turned it into a successful hotel after he had fallen on hard times. Although a hotel, it still had all the air of a comfortable Highland country house, and Patricia felt at home there.

She began to feel better as she sat down in the dining room and looked around. The month was June, and after a grim winter and icy spring, when Siberian winds had blown from the east, bringing blizzards and chilblains, the wind had suddenly shifted to the west, carrying the foretaste of better weather to come.

The dining room was quite full. A noisy

4

fishing party dominated the main table in the centre of the room, Patricia's kind of people but oblivious to one lonely spinster in the corner.

Then waitresses came in and began to bustle about, putting the remaining tables together to form one large one. A coach party entered, noisy and flushed, and took places round this table. Patricia frowned. Who would have thought that the Tommel Castle Hotel would allow a coach party?

The fact was that the colonel was away with his wife visiting friends, his daughter was in London and the manager, Mr Johnson, had decided that a party of middle-aged tourists could do no harm.

Patricia had just finished her soup and was wishing she had the courage to cancel the rest of her order when a tall, lanky man came into the dining room and stood looking around. He had flaming red hair and intelligent hazel eyes. His suit was well cut and he wore a snowy-white shirt and silk tie. But with it, he was wearing a large pair of ugly boots.

The maître d' went up to him and Patricia heard him say sourly, 'We have no tables left, Macbeth.'

'Mr Macbeth to you, Jenkins,' she heard the man with the red hair say in a light, amused voice. 'I'm sure you'll have a table soon.'

They had both moved into the dining room and were standing beside Patricia's table.

'No, not for a long time,' said the maître d'.

The man called Macbeth suddenly saw Patricia watching him and gave her a smile.

Patricia could not quite believe the sound of her own voice, but she heard herself saying stiffly, 'The gentleman can share my table if he wishes.'

'That will not be necessary . . .' began Jenkins, but the red-haired man promptly sat down opposite her.

'Run along, Jenkins,' he said, 'and glare at someone else.'

Hamish Macbeth turned to Patricia. 'This is verra kind of you.'

She regretted her invitation and wished she had brought a book with her.

'I am Hamish Macbeth,' he said with another of those charming smiles. 'I am the village policeman in Lochdubh, and you are Miss Patricia Martyn-Broyd and you live over by Cnothan.'

'I did not think we had met,' said Patricia.

'We haven't,' said Hamish. 'But you know what the Highlands are like. Everyone knows everyone else. I heard you had been away.' He took the menu from a hovering waitress as he spoke. He scanned it quickly. 'I'll have the soup and the trout,' he said.

'I have just come back from Greece,' said Patricia. 'Do you know Greece?'

'I don't know much of anywhere except the Highlands of Scotland,' said Hamish ruefully.

'I'm an armchair traveller. I am surprised you stayed up here so long.'

'Why?' asked Patricia.

'It can be a lonely place. Usually the English we get are drunks or romantics, and I would say you do not fall into either category.'

'Hardly,' said Patricia with a fluting, humorless laugh. 'I am a writer.'

'Of what?'

'Detective stories.'

'I read a lot o' those,' said Hamish. 'You must write under another name.'

'I regret to say my books have been out of print for some time.'

'Ah, well,' said Hamish awkwardly. 'I am sure you will find the inspiration up here.'

'I hardly think the county of Sutherland is overrun with criminals.'

'I meant, it's a funny landscape which can produce the weird fancies.'

'My last detective story was set in Scotland, but the others, mainly in the south, were village mysteries.'

'Like Agatha Christie?'

'A little better crafted, if I may say so,' said Patricia, again with that irritating laugh of hers.

'Then it iss the miracle that yours are out o' print,' said Hamish maliciously.

'It is not my fault. I had a useless publisher, who would not promote them properly, and a worse agent,' snapped Patricia, and then, to her horror, she began to cry.

'There, now,' said Hamish. 'Don't greet. You havenae settled down after all the travel, and it's been a grim winter. I would like to read one o' your books.'

Patricia produced a small, white, starched handkerchief from her handbag and wiped her eyes and blew her nose.

'I think I am too out of touch with the modern world to write a detective story again,' she said, all the time wondering why she was confiding in a village policeman.

'I could help you wi' a wee bit of information, if you like.'

'That's very kind of you. But I do not think it would do much good. I've tried to write another one with a Highland background, but my mind seems set in England.'

'Perhaps you should get to know a few of us better,' said Hamish, 'and then it might come easier.'

'Perhaps,' she echoed sadly.

'Although, if I may point out,' said Hamish cautiously, 'Cnothan is not the friendliest village in the place. In fact, I would say it's a sour little dump.'

She gave him a watery smile. 'Not like Lochdubh?'

'There's nowhere like Lochdubh,' said Hamish stoutly. 'Maybe if you stopped writing for a bit, it would all come back. Do you fish?'

'I still have my rods, but I haven't done any fishing for a long time.'

Somewhere in Hamish's head a warning bell was beginning to clang, telling him to stay away from lame ducks in general and this woman in particular, who had been locally damned as an 'awfy auld snob'. But he said, 'I hae the day off tomorrow. I'll take ye out on the Anstey if ye want.'

This met with Patricia's ideas of what was right and fitting. Fishing on a Scottish river with a policeman as ghillie was socially acceptable to her mind.

'Thank you,' she said. 'I will need a permit.'

Hamish shifted uneasily. 'Oh, I'll see to that. Pick you up at nine in the morning.'

They chatted pleasantly through the rest of the meal, Hamish amiably but Patricia betraying with each further sentence the awful rigidity of her attitudes.

They separated at the end of the meal, each with different thoughts; Hamish regretting his generous gesture and Patricia feeling quite elated. Hamish Macbeth was really quite intelligent, she thought. It was a shame he was only a village policeman. Perhaps with her help he could make something of himself. And so Patricia drove happily homewards, not knowing she had joined the long list of women who thought they could change one contented, unambitious Highland constable.

* * *

9

She felt the glorious blustery morning that dawned was a good omen. But nine o'clock came and went and she began to feel panicky. If Hamish did not come, then it meant slipping back into that depressing isolation which had become her way of life.

And then at half past nine, she saw to her relief a police Land Rover lurching over the potholes in the road, a fishing rod sticking out of the window.

She went out to meet him. 'Sorry I'm late,' said Hamish. 'Have you got waders? I forgot to ask.'

'Yes, although I haven't used them for some time. I hope they're still waterproof,' said Patricia.

'We'll take your car if you don't mind,' said Hamish. 'I'm not really supposed to drive people around in a police car unless I'm arresting them.'

Soon they were fishing on the river Anstey. The mountaintops were clear against a blue sky for the first time in months. Patricia found to her delight that she had lost none of her old skill. She was just about to suggest a break for lunch when the enterprising constable said he had brought along a picnic. Patricia had caught two trout and Hamish one.

'Afore we have our food, I would suggest we pack everything up and put it in the boot o' your car,' said Hamish.

'But why?' She felt sharply disappointed. 'I hoped we would have some more fishing.'

Hamish looked around, scanning the river-banks and the surrounding hillsides. 'Aye, well, we'll do that, but chust let's put the stuff away.'

They stripped off their waders and dis-mantled their rods and put all the fishing impedimenta in the boot of Patricia's car.

Hamish produced a picnic basket from which he removed thick chicken sandwiches and a flask of coffee.

They were sitting on a flat rock beside the river when a truculent voice behind them said, 'I hope ye havenae been fishing this river, Macbeth.'

'Oh, it iss yourself, Willie,' said Hamish without turning around. 'No, no, Miss Martyn-Broyd and myself was chust having the picnic.'

Patricia swung round, her mouth full of sandwich.

'Willie MacPhee, the water bailiff,' said Hamish, his eyes signalling a warning.

Willie was a thick-set man with beetling brows in a red weather-beaten face. He had a heavy round chin, but his head tapered to a narrow crown, giving the appearance of a face seen reflected in a shiny balloon.

He lumbered up to Patricia's car and peered in the windows. Patricia's heart beat hard. All at once she knew Hamish's reason for shutting all the fishing stuff up in the boot. He did not have a fishing permit!

Willie came back and stood over them. 'I hope ye know, missus,' he said, addressing Patricia, 'that ye cannae fish the Anstey without a permit.'

The daughter of the land agent felt quite queasy. She wondered why she had never stopped to consider how a Highland policeman could even afford the probably horrendous price of a fishing permit. But she did not like being loomed over.

Miss Patricia Martyn-Broyd got to her feet.

'Are you accusing me of *poaching*, my good man?' she demanded in glacial tones.

Willie gave an odd, ducking movement of his head, like a dog backing down before a more powerful adversary.

'Just making sure,' he said sulkily. 'Macbeth here has no respect for the law.'

With that, he lumbered off.

Patricia waited until she was sure he was out of earshot and then rounded on Hamish. 'How could you? And you a policeman.'

'Well, I'm a Highlander as well, and it iss considered no crime up here to take a fish from the river.'

'If it is no crime, then why do they have game laws and why do they have water bailiffs?'

'That,' said Hamish, unrepentant, 'is to add a spice o' danger to the sport. We'll just enjoy our meal and try the river again.'

12

'Are you mad? I, for one, do not want to appear in a Scottish sheriff's court.'

'He won't be back,' said Hamish cheerfully. 'He's lazy. He only picks on easy targets.'

Patricia was about to suggest sternly that she return home immediately, but in that moment a picture of her windswept cottage arose in her mind's eye. Having broken out of her long isolation, she was reluctant to go back to it.

She gave a weak smile. 'You are a terrible man. You must be in your thirties and yet you are still only a policeman. Is that because you have little respect for the law?'

'Except for the fishing, I haff the great respect for the law,' said Hamish. 'But I like Lochdubh and I hate Strathbane, which is where I would have to go if I got promoted.'

'But everyone is ambitious.'

'And not everyone is happy. You are looking at the exception to the rule.'

They fished all afternoon in the warm sunlight without catching anything else, but Patricia enjoyed herself immensely. At the end of the day, she invited Hamish to join her for dinner, but he said he had reports to type up. Patricia wanted to ask if she could see him again but felt as shy and tongue-tied as a teenager and just as frightened of rejection.

Hamish, with that almost telepathic ability of the Highlander, was well aware of what was going through her mind. She hadn't been bad company, he thought. Maybe she would now branch out a bit. *Don't get involved*, screamed his mind. *She's all right, but she's a bit rigid and pompous, and if she's lonely, it is all her own damned fault.* But he found himself saying weakly as he climbed out of her car, 'Perhaps I could help ye with some ideas for a detective story? Maybe we could hae a bit o' dinner tomorrow night.'

Her face glowed. 'That is very kind of you, but let it be my treat. Where would you like to go?'

'The Napoli, that Italian restaurant in Lochdubh.'

'Very well,' said Patricia happily. 'I will see you at eight o'clock.'

She turned and went indoors. She scooped the post up from the doormat. The postman had delivered her mail that day after she had left. She carried the letters in and dropped them on the table in the living room. She never received anything interesting through the post. It was usually bank statements and junk mail.

She hummed to herself as she made a cup of tea. She carried it through to her little living room cum dining room and sat down at the table.

Then she found there was a letter with the legend 'Strathclyde Television' on the envelope. She slowly opened it.

'Dear Ms Martyn-Broyd,' she read. 'We have had the delight of reading some of your detective stories and are interested in making some

14

of them into a series, possibly starting with *The Case of the Rising Tides*. We would be happy to deal with you through your agent if you could supply us with a name, address and telephone number. In any case, please telephone so that I can arrange to meet you to discuss this project. Yours sincerely, Harry Frame, Executive Producer, Strathclyde Television.'

Patricia read the letter several times and then slowly put it down with a shaking hand. After all these long years, recognition at last!

She passed a night of broken sleep and was awake by dawn, waiting and waiting until such time as offices opened and she could begin to make telephone calls.

She had to wait until ten o'clock before she was finally able to talk to Harry Frame.

'This is a pleasure,' he boomed. 'May I call you Patricia?'

'Please do ... Harry.' Patricia felt she had just made an exciting leap into an exciting, modern world.

'Would you have any objection to us dramatizing your books?'

'I am very flattered,' fluted Patricia. 'Who will play Lady Harriet?'

'Early days, early days. Perhaps you could visit us in Glasgow so we may discuss the terms of the contract? Or perhaps you would like me to contact your agent?'

Patricia felt a sudden burst of hatred for her ex-agent, who had done nothing to stop her precious books going out of print.

'No,' she said firmly, 'I will handle the negotiations myself.'

And so the arrangements were made. The day was Wednesday. On Friday Patricia would take the early train from Inverness to Perth and then the train from Perth to Glasgow, where a taxi would be waiting to bear her to Strathclyde Television.

By the time she put down the phone, her face was flushed and her heart beating hard.

Then, after another restorative cup of coffee, she dialled her old publishers and asked to speak to her former editor, Brian Jones, only to find that Mr Jones was dead. She explained the reason for her call and was put through to a woman editor, Jessica Durnham. Patricia explained about the television series. To her disappointment, her news was not met with an offer of thousands for the reissue of all her books. The editor said cautiously that she would discuss it at conference and get back to her, or perhaps phone her agent? 'No, you will deal with me,' said Patricia firmly.

She spent the rest of the day in rosy dreams, and it was only as evening approached that she remembered her date with the village constable.

She frowned. She should not have gone slumming with a policeman. Good heavens!

What if that water bailiff had caught her and she had ended up in court? A celebrity such as Patricia Martyn-Broyd must be very careful of her reputation. She telephoned the police station and left a curt message on the answering machine.

Hamish had been visiting his parents in Rogart and had then gone straight to the restaurant on his return and so did not receive the message until after he had eaten a solitary meal.

The voice on his answering machine was almost offensively curt. He shrugged. He probably wouldn't see her again, and that was no great loss.

Half an hour before Patricia was due to arrive at Strathclyde Television, Harry Frame was chairing a conference. Several people sat around the table, each clutching a copy of *The Case of the Rising Tides*. They had been able to get only one of the books and had run off copies.

'You want me to produce this?' demanded Fiona King, a rawboned, chain-smoking woman dressed in the height of lesbian chic: bone-short haircut, short jersey exposing an area of yellow skin at the midriff, jeans and large combat boots. 'It will be an interesting

17

challenge.' Privately she thought it the most boring load of crap she had ever been forced to read, but surely something could be done with it.

'The thing about it is this,' said Harry wearily. 'She's been out of print for ages, so she won't cost much. We set it in the sixties, flares and white boots and miniskirts.'

'Is this going to be Sunday night family viewing?' demanded Fiona, lighting another cigarette despite the NO SMOKING sign above her head. 'You know, the sort of pap the cocoa-slurping morons of middle Britain enjoy?'

'Yes,' said Harry. 'But we're still going in for shock here. Lots of bonking.'

'But this bitch, Lady Harriet, definitely keeps her Harris tweed knickers on right through the book.'

'We'll get 'em off, give her a bit of rough stuff to roll in the heather with.'

'What setting will you have?' asked a researcher.

'Plenty of places in the Highlands.'

'And who'll play Lady Harriet?'

'Penelope Gates.'

'Jesus,' said Fiona. 'That foul-mouthed little keelie.'

'She's got great tits, and she's prepared to open her legs on television.'

'And off television,' remarked Fiona sourly. 'What on earth is this old frump Martyn-Broyd going to say?'

'We just get her to sign. After that, she'll just need to lump it. In fact, she'll enjoy it. Everyone these days wants to have something to do with television. Have you seen those schlock TV shows from the States? They'll divorce their hubby on screen if it gets them a few moments of fame. I don't like your tone, Fiona. Don't you want to do this?'

'I consider it a privilege to be chosen by you, Harry,' said Fiona quickly.

A secretary popped her head round the door and said primly, 'Miss Martyn-Broyd is here.'

Patricia entered, looking flustered. There had been no taxi to meet her at the station. Every television company was notorious for failing to meet people at airports and stations, but Patricia did not know this and took the absence of a waiting taxi to be a sort of snub.

Furthermore, she had expected something glossier, not this concrete slab of a building situated under a motorway, which seemed to be furnished with stained carpet and plastic plants.

She had been handed a plastic name tag at the reception desk to pin on her tweed suit, but she had angrily stuffed it into her handbag on her way up. It had reminded her of a dreadful American party she had gone to years before, where she had been given a name tag to pin on her dress with the legend 'Hi! My name is Patricia', and she still shuddered at the memory.

Sheila Burford, a research assistant, looked up curiously at Patricia. That's a medieval face, she thought, looking at the hooded pale eyes in the white face and the curved nose.

Harry Frame greeted Patricia by kissing her on the cheek, an embrace from which Patricia visibly winced.

Patricia was as disappointed in Harry Frame as she was in the building. He was a big man with a mane of brown hair and a puffy face. He was wearing a checked workman's shirt open nearly to the waist, and he had a great mat of chest hair.

'Sit yourself down, Patricia,' he boomed. 'Tea? Coffee? Drink?'

'No, I thank you,' said Patricia. 'I would like to get down to business.'

'I like a businesswoman,' said Harry expansively. He introduced her all round, ending up with, 'And this is Fiona King, who will be our producer.'

Patricia concealed her dismay. 'I am not familiar with your television company, Mr Frame. What successes have you had?'

'I have them written down for you,' said Harry, handing her a list.

Patricia looked down at the list in bewilderment. They seemed to be mostly documentaries with titles like *Whither Scotland?*, *Are the English Bastards?*, *The Arguments for Home Rule*, *The Highland Clearances*, *Folk Songs from the Gorbals*. She had not seen or heard of any of them.

'I do not see any detective stories here,' said Patricia.

Harry ignored that. 'Because of this your books will be back in print,' he said. 'We suggest a publicity tie-up with Pheasant Books. We plan to start serializing *The Case of the Rising Tides*.'

Patricia stared at him unnervingly. Then she suddenly smiled. From being a rather tatty building inhabited with people who were definitely not ladies and gentlemen, Strathclyde Television and all in it became suffused with a golden glow. She barely heard anything of the further discussion. She did, however, agree to signing an option contract for a thousand pounds and accepting an agreement that if the series were sold to the BBC or ITV or anyone else, she would receive two thousand pounds per episode. Money was not important to Patricia, who was comfortably off, but the thought of getting her precious books back into print made her pretty much deaf to other concerns.

Business being done, Fiona and Harry said they would take Patricia out for lunch. As they ushered her towards the door, Harry glanced down the table to where Sheila Burford was making notes. Sheila had cropped blonde hair, large blue eyes and a splendid figure which her outfit of bomber jacket and jeans could not quite hide. 'You'd best come along as well, Sheila,' said Harry.

They took her to a restaurant across from the television centre. It was called Tatty Tommy's Tartan Howf and was scented with the aroma of old cooking fat. They were served by Tatty Tommy himself, a large bruiser with a shaved head, an earring and blue eye shadow.

Patricia was disappointed. She had thought that a television company would have taken her to some Glaswegian equivalent of the Ritz. She bleakly ordered Tatty Tommy's Tumshies, Tatties and Haggis, thinking that an ethnic dish of haggis, turnips and potatoes might be safer than some of the more exotic offerings on the menu; but it transpired that the haggis was as dry as bone, the turnips watery and the potatoes had that chemical flavour of the reconstituted packet kind.

'In my book,' said Patricia, 'the setting is a fictitious village called Duncraggie.'

'Oh, we'll be setting it in the Highlands,' said Fiona brightly. 'Pretty setting and lots of good Scottish actors.'

'But the characters are *English*!' protested Patricia. 'It is a house party in the Highlands. Lady Harriet is Scottish, yes, but educated in England.'

Harry waved an expansive arm. 'English, Scottish, we're all British.'

Sheila repressed a smile. Harry was a vehement campaigner for Scotland's independence.

'I suppose,' began Patricia again, but Harry put a bearlike arm about her shoulders.

22

'Now, don't you be worrying your head about the television side. Just think how grand it will be to see your books on the shelves again.'

He had shrewdly guessed that, at that moment in time, Patricia would agree to anything just so long as she got her books published.

'Who will play the lead?' asked Patricia. 'I thought of Diana Rigg.'

'Bit old now,' said Fiona. 'We thought of Penelope Gates.'

'I have never heard of her,' said Patricia, pushing her plate away with most of the food on it uneaten.

'Oh, she's up and coming,' said Fiona.

And cheap, reflected Sheila cynically.

'Have I seen her in anything?'

Fiona and Harry exchanged quick glances. 'Do you watch television much?' asked Fiona.

'Hardly at all.'

'Oh, if you had,' said Fiona, 'you would have seen a lot of her.'

And most of it naked, thought Sheila. Scotland's answer to Sharon Stone.

Sheila did not like Patricia much but was beginning to feel sorry for this old lady. She had asked Harry why on earth choose some old bat's out-of-print books when they meant to pay scant attention to characters or plot, and Harry had replied that respectability spiced up with sex was a winner. Besides, the book they

23

meant to serialize was set in the sixties, and he planned to have lots of flared trousers, wide lapels, Mary Quant dresses and espresso bars, despite the fact that the fashions of the sixties had passed Patricia by.

Patricia's head was beginning to ache. She wanted to escape from this bad and smelly restaurant and these odd people. All would be well when she was back home and could savour in privacy all the delights of the prospect of being back in print.

They asked the usual polite questions that writers get asked: How do you think of your plots? Do you have a writing schedule? Patricia answered, all the time trying to remember what it had really been like to sit down each morning and get to work.

At last, when the lunch was over, Patricia consulted her timetable and said there was a train in half an hour. 'Sheila here will get you a cab and take you to the station,' said Harry.

Patricia shook hands all round. Sheila had run out and hailed a cab while Patricia was making her farewells.

'It must all seem a bit bewildering,' said Sheila as they headed for the station.

'Yes, it is rather,' drawled Patricia, leaning back in the cab and feeling very important now that freedom was at hand. 'When will I hear from you again?'

'It takes time,' said Sheila. 'First we have to find the main scriptwriter, choose the location, the actors, and then we sell it to either the BBC or ITV.'

'The BBC would be wonderful,' said Patricia. 'Don't like the other channel. All those nasty advertisements. So vulgar.'

'In any case, it will take a few months,' said Sheila.

'Did you read *The Case of the Rising Tides*?' asked Patricia.

'Yes, it was part of my job as researcher. I enjoyed it very much,' said Sheila, who had found it boring in the extreme.

'I pay great attention to detail,' said Patricia importantly.

'I noticed that,' said Sheila, remembering long paragraphs of detailed descriptions of high and low tides. 'Didn't Dorothy Sayers use a bit about tides in *Have His Carcase*?'

Patricia gave a patronizing little laugh. 'I often found Miss Sayers's plots a trifle *loose.*' And Dorothy Sayers is long dead and I am alive and my books are going to be on television, she thought with a sudden rush of elation.

She said goodbye to Sheila at the station, thinking that it was a pity such a pretty girl should wear such odd and dreary clothes.

Sheila walked thoughtfully away down the platform after having seen her charge ensconced in a corner seat. She scratched her short blonde crop. Did Harry realize just how vain Patricia Martyn-Broyd was? But then he had endured fights with writers before. Writers were considered the scum of the earth.

At a conference a week later, Harry announced, 'I'm waiting for Jamie Gallagher. He'll be main scriptwriter. I gave him the book. He'll be coming along to let us know what he can do with it.'

'I wouldn't have thought he was at all suitable,' suggested Sheila. 'Not for a detective series.'

'BBC Scotland likes his work, and if we want them to put up any money for this, we'd better give 'em what they want,' said Harry.

The door opened and Jamie Gallagher came in. He was a tall man wearing a donkey jacket and a Greek fisherman's hat. He had a few days of stubble on his chin. He had greasy brown hair which he wore combed forward to hide his receding hairline. He was a heavy drinker, and his face was criss-crossed with broken veins. It looked like an ordnance survey map.

He threw a tattered copy of Patricia's book down on the table and demanded truculently, 'What is this shite?'

'Well, shite, actually,' said Harry cheerfully, 'but we need you to bring all that genius of yours to it.'

Jamie sat down and scowled all around. He was battling between the joys of exercising his monumental ego on the one hand and remembering that he was currently unemployed on the other.

'What you need to do is take the framework of the plot, all those tides and things,' said Fiona, 'and then add some spice.'

After a long harangue about the English in general and Patricia's writing in particular, Jamie said, 'But I could do it this way. You say we'll get Penelope Gates? Right. You want the sixties feel. Lots of sixties songs. In the books, Lady Harriet is middle-aged. I say, let's make her young and hip. I know, runs a commune in that castle of hers. Bit of pot. Love interest.'

'In the book,' said Sheila, 'it's Major Derwent.'

'Let's see,' said Jamie, ignoring her, 'we'll have a Highland police inspector, real chauvinist pig. And our Harriet seduces him and gets information about the case out of him. Lots of shagging in the heather.'

'We won't get the family slot on Sunday night,' said Fiona cautiously.

Jamie snorted. 'We'll get it, all right. Who the hell is going to object to pot smoking these days? No full frontal, either, just a flash of thigh and a bit of boob.'

Sheila let her mind drift off. Poor Patricia up in the Highlands, dreaming of glory. What on earth would she think when she saw the result? The air about Sheila was blue with

27

four-letter words, but she had become accustomed to bleeping them out. Someone had once said that you could always tell what people were afraid of by the swear words they used.

After six months Patricia began to become anxious. What if nothing happened? Pheasant Books had not phoned her, and she was too proud and, at the same time, too afraid of rejection to phone them. She had not heard from her old publisher, either.

The Highlands were in the grip of deep mid-winter. There was hardly any daylight, and she seemed to be living in a long tunnel of perpetual night.

She began to regret that she had not furthered her friendship with that policeman over in Lochdubh. It would have been someone to talk to. She had diligently tried to write again, but somehow the words would not come.

At last she phoned the police station in Lochdubh. When Hamish answered, she said, 'This is Patricia Martyn-Broyd. Do you remember me?'

'Oh, yes, you stood me up,' said Hamish cheerfully.

'I am sorry, but you see . . .' She told Hamish all about the television deal, ending with a cautious, 'Perhaps you might be free for dinner tomorrow night?'

'Aye, that would be grand,' said Hamish. 'That Italian restaurant?'

'I will see you there at eight,' said Patricia.


But on the following day, the outside world burst in on Patricia's seclusion. Harry Frame phoned to tell her he had got funding for the series.

'From the BBC?' asked Patricia eagerly.

'Yes,' said Harry, 'BBC Scotland.'

'Not national?'

'Oh, it will go national all right,' Harry gave his beefy laugh. 'The fact that we're going to dramatize your books has already been in some of the papers. Haven't you seen anything?'

Patricia took *The Times*, but she only read the obituaries and did the crossword. She wondered, however, why no reporter had contacted her.

'We're sending you the contracts,' said Harry. 'You should get them tomorrow.'

Then Pheasant Books phoned to say they would like to publish *The Case of the Rising Tides* to coincide with the start of the television series. They offered a dismal amount of money, but Patricia was too happy to care. She took a deep breath and said she would travel down to London immediately to sign the contract.

She packed quickly and drove down to Inverness to catch the London train.

Hamish Macbeth sat alone in the restaurant that evening. Crazy old bat, he thought.

# Chapter Two

*Oh! how many torments lie in the small circle
of a wedding-ring!*

– Colley Cibber

Penelope Gates stood for a moment at the bottom of the staircase leading up to the flat she shared with her husband. She wondered for the umpteenth time why she had been stupid enough to get married. No one got married these days. Her husband, Josh, was an out-of-work actor and bitter with it. To justify his existence, he had lately taken to acting as a sort of business manager, criticizing her scripts and performance. They had first met when both were students at the Royal College of Dramatic Art in Glasgow. It had been a heady three-week romance followed by a wedding.

The first rows had begun when Penelope had acted in a television series as a rape victim. Josh, when he got drunk, which was frequently, accused her of being a slut. Only the fact that he liked the money she earned from subsequent and similar roles had stopped him from outright violence, had stopped him from 'damaging the goods'. But the last time, he had extracted a promise from her that she would never take her clothes off on screen again, and, anything for a quiet life, thought Penelope bleakly, she had promised. Maybe she could get away with it this time. She nervously thumbed the script of *The Case of the Rising Tides*. She was not *totally* naked in any scene.

Penelope went upstairs and opened the door. 'Josh!' she called. 'I've got a great part.'

His voice sounded from the kitchen, slightly slurred. 'What filth are you going to act in now?'

'Not filth,' said Penelope. 'Sunday night viewing. Detective series.' She had thrust the script into her briefcase on the way to the kitchen. She took out a battered copy of *The Case of the Rising Tides* and handed it to him. 'It's based on this.'

He took it and scowled down at it. After this, I'll have enough money to run away, thought Penelope. What did I ever see in him?

Josh was a heavyset young man with thick black hair and a square, handsome face, but one that was becoming blurred with drink. His mouth seemed set in a permanent sneer.

She made herself a cup of tea and stood by the window, cradling the cup in her hands. A flock of pigeons soared up into the windy sky above Great Western Road. Women's lib was a farce, she thought. Women were not as strong as men, whatever anyone said. Again she felt trapped, suffocated.

At last she heard Josh's voice behind her, mollified, almost gentle. 'Aye, it looks as if you've hit the jackpot this time, lass. It's a wee bittie old-fashioned. I've only read the first few pages. Are you playing this Lady Harriet?'

'Yes, the main part,' said Penelope, turning around.

'It could be like that Miss Marple,' said Josh, his eyes glowing. 'It could run forever. Got the script?'

'They're so frightened of the opposition that they lock the scripts up at Strathclyde Television,' lied Penelope.

'I'm happy for you,' said Josh, 'and you should be happy for yourself. I'm telling you, lass, if you'd bared your body on another show, I'd have strangled you.' His eyes gleamed wetly with threat and drink.

Penelope gave a nervous little laugh. 'You don't mean that.'

'Don't I just. Let's go out and celebrate. What's the location?'

'I don't know yet. They're up in the Highlands looking for one.'


The Strathclyde Television van cruised slowly through the snowy roads of Sutherland. It was not actually snowing, but a vicious wind was

33

blowing little blizzards across their vision from the snowy fields on either side of the road, where occasionally the humped figures of sheep could be seen.

'Why this far north?' asked Fiona King from the depths of a down-padded jacket. 'I still say we could have found somewhere out in the Trossachs, about half an hour's drive from Glasgow.'

'Loch Lomond's too crowded, and you'd have too many tourists gawking,' said Jamie Gallagher. He, Fiona and Sheila had been sent out to choose a location. They had zigzagged across Scotland on their way up. Fiona and Sheila had thought they had found various good locations, but Jamie had turned them all down. And as he was the favoured one with BBC Scotland, they both knew they had to let him make the final choice.

Sheila was driving. She was tired and worried about the state of the roads, worried about skidding into a drift. It was such a bleak, white landscape.

And then the wind suddenly dropped. Up ahead of her on the winding road, a shaft of sunlight struck down. She fished out a pair of sunglasses and put them on to protect her eyes against the glare.

'There's a village down there,' she said. 'Let's stop for something. I could do with a cup of tea.'

'We'll see,' said Jamie huffily. 'But remember your job's to look for a location.'

'It's called Lochdubh,' said Sheila, reading the sign. 'Oh, this might do.'

She swung the large van over a hump-backed bridge.

Snowy Lochdubh lay spread out before them in the winter sunlight. A line of small cottages faced the waterfront. There was a harbour and a square grey church, and above the village soared two enormous mountains.

'There's a police station,' said Jamie. 'Pull up there, Sheila.'

'Why?'

'Just do as you're told!'

Sheila pulled up beside the police station. They all got down.

'There's someone in the kitchen,' said Jamie. He knocked on the door.

A tall, red-haired man answered the door, wiping his hands on a dishcloth. He was wearing an old blue wool sweater over a checked shirt, but his thick trousers were regulation black, as were his large boots.

'Are you the policeman?' asked Jamie.

'Aye, I'm Hamish Macbeth. What brings you?'

'Can we come in?' Jamie asked, shivering. 'It's damn cold.'

'Come ben.' Hamish turned and led the way through to his living room. 'Would you like tea or coffee?'

Sheila smiled. 'That would be lovely. Coffee, please.'

'Forget it,' snarled Jamie. 'We've business here.'

'Let's have it, then,' said Hamish, taking a dislike to him.

'We're from Strathclyde Television, and we're up here looking for a location. We're filming a detective series.'

'That would be Miss Martyn-Broyd's book,' said Hamish 'What about here? You won't find a prettier place.'

'Not right. Too bourgeois,' said Jamie.

Hamish raised his eyebrows. 'I havenae heard that word in years. How much time have you spent in Lochdubh?'

'We've just arrived.'

'Snap judgement?'

'I always make snap judgements,' said Jamie. 'I can get the feel and smell o' a place in one minute flat.'

'We've a lot in common,' said Hamish Macbeth. 'I can get the smell and feel o' a person in one minute flat.'

He took out a handkerchief and held it to his nose. Sheila suppressed a grin.

'So why we're here is to find out if you've any suggestions.'

'I can't think without a cup of coffee,' said Hamish amiably. 'I'll get you one while I'm at it, Miss . . .?'

'Sheila. Sheila Burford. I'll come and help you.'

She followed him through to the kitchen. 'Look,' said Sheila urgently, 'think of something. I've been driving and driving.'

'Who is he? The producer?'

'No, the scriptwriter. Fiona's the producer.'

'So how come he's calling the shots?'

'BBC Scotland are funding it, and Jamie's their favourite scriptwriter.'

'I'm surprised somebody loves him,' said Hamish dryly. 'Do you think thon Fiona-woman would like a cup?'

'No, she crawls to Jamie,' said Sheila, wondering why she was chatting so openly with a Highland policeman.

He handed her a mug of coffee. 'I'll see what I can do.'

They returned to the living room.

Hamish sat down and smiled sweetly at Jamie. 'I believe I haff chust thought of the very place for you.'

Sheila was to learn that the sudden sibilancy of Hamish's Highland accent meant he was annoyed or upset.

'Where's that?' asked Jamie.

'It's a place called Drim, not far from here.'

'And what's so good about it?'

'It's an odd place. It's at the end of a sea loch. The whole place is sinister.'

'We need a castle,' said Jamie. 'The main character's supposed to live in a castle.'

'Five miles on the far side o' Drim is Drim Castle, owned by Major Neal. He'd rented it to an American who's just packed up and left. I think all the furniture's been put back in storage.'

'Doesn't matter,' said Fiona, speaking for the first time. She blew out a cloud of smoke. 'We could use it as offices as well as location.'

'Aye, well, there you are. Drim's your place.'

'Then we'll go and have a look. Come along, Sheila, and stop slurping coffee and do your job.'

Sheila threw Hamish an apologetic smile.

Hamish followed them out and gave Sheila directions. He waved them goodbye and then went indoors to phone Major Neal. 'Make sure you get a good price,' he cautioned after explaining what it was all about.

'I'll do that,' said the major. 'I owe you one, Hamish.'

'Won't forget it.' Hamish said goodbye. As far as he was concerned, Drim and Jamie deserved each other. He had once solved a murder there, but although Drim was on his beat, he went there as little as possible.

'What about Plockton in Ross?' asked Fiona, finally breaking the silence as they drove towards Drim.

'Plockton!' sneered Jamie. 'Thon village has been used in two detective series already.'

'I think that's it down there,' said Sheila.

Drim was a small huddle of cottages on a flat piece of land surrounded by towering mountains at the end of a thin, narrow sea loch. There was a church and a community hall and a general store, and the road down to the village was a precipitous single-track.

'It'll be hell getting all the stuff here,' muttered Fiona.

Shafts of late red sunlight shone down, cutting through the crevices in the mountains, flooding Drim with a red light. Sheila thought it looked like a village in hell.

'Bypass the village and let's see this castle before the light fades,' ordered Jamie.

Sheila would have missed the turn had not the major stationed two of his gamekeepers out on the road to direct them. She drove cautiously up a snow-covered drive, stalling from time to time, wheels spinning on the ice, until at last the castle came into view.

The last of the red light was flooding the front. It was a Gothic building, built during the height of the Victorian vogue for homes in the Highlands. It even had a mock drawbridge and portcullis, but no moat, the first owner having run out of money before one could be dug.

The major met them at the door. He was a small, neat man, dressed in old tweeds. He had a pleasant, lined face and faded blue eyes.

'Macbeth phoned me to say you might be calling,' said the major. 'Come in.'

He had lit an enormous fire in the huge fireplace in the hall and had arranged chairs and a low table in front of it, on which he had placed a bottle of whisky and glasses.

They introduced themselves. The bullying side of Jamie would have liked to dismiss the whole of Drim as a possible location and make Sheila drive on, but the sight of that bottle of whisky mellowed him. Sheila did not drink because she was driving. Fiona did not drink alcohol. She thought it a dangerous drug. She smoked pot and was part of an organization to get the use of cannabis legalized. So Jamie had most of the bottle.

The major, who had read Patricia's book *The Case of the Rising Tides*, was becoming more and more amused as Jamie waxed enthusiastic over his planned dramatization of the book.

At last, exhausted by talking and bragging and drinking, he fell asleep and Fiona took over and got down to the nitty-gritty of price. She ended up agreeing to pay more than she had intended because she was weary of travelling and the castle was suitable for film offices as well as a location and the major seemed so eager to help.

At last, business being finished, and when Sheila had taken photographs of all the rooms, he directed them back to Lochdubh and suggested they stay at the Tommel Castle Hotel for the night.

Jamie was roused from his slumbers. He was in a foul temper all the way back to Lochdubh, and once checked into the hotel, he headed straight for the bar.

Fiona phoned Harry Frame in Glasgow. 'It's Drim,' she said wearily.

'Where the hell's that?' asked Harry.

'It's at the ends of the earth,' said Fiona, 'but Jamie's happy and it's right in every way.' She began to enthuse over the castle, deliberately not mentioning the awkward business of getting there.


Major Neal said to his head gamekeeper, 'You'll find a good haunch of venison in the freezer and a side of smoked salmon. Take them over to Macbeth at Lochdubh tomorrow with my thanks. No, forget it. I haven't seen Hamish in ages. I'll take them over myself.'

'That's very good of you,' beamed Hamish when the major arrived on his doorstep half an hour later, bearing gifts.

'Least I could do, Hamish,' said the major, following him into the kitchen. 'But, oh my, what's Miss Martyn-Broyd going to do when she hears how they're planning to change her book?'

'What are they going to do with it? A dram?'

'Just the one, Hamish.' They both sat down at the kitchen table. 'It's like this. . . . Have you read *The Case of the Rising Tides*?'

Hamish shook his head.

'It's not bad. Complicated plot. But it's a lady's book, if you know what I mean. The main character is a Scottish aristocrat called Lady Harriet Vere.'

'So her father was an earl or something like that?'

'The author doesn't mention any parents at all. Just this Lady Harriet who lives in a castle in the Highlands with devoted servants. In the TV series, she's going to drop a few years – in the book she's around forty, with a stern, handsome face and so on – and be played by Penelope Gates, who is a voluptuous blonde whose recent performances on the box have left nothing to the imagination. Unless she dyes her pubic hair as well, she's a real blonde.'

'You'd make a good detective,' said Hamish dryly.

'Anyway, in the TV series, she's going to be a hippie aristocrat who runs a commune in her castle, pot and free love.'

'Bit sixties.'

'It's set in the sixties.'

'I wonder if Miss Martyn-Broyd knows this,' said Hamish.

'Probably does. Her books have been out of print. Bound to go along with anything. I'll be glad when the light nights come back again, Hamish. These long northern winters get me down. But thanks to you, once they start filming and I get paid, I'll be able to take a holiday somewhere far away from Scotland.'

'Nonetheless, I wouldn't tell Miss Martyn-Broyd about what they're going to do to her book, in case she doesn't know. Better to upset her later than sooner. How are things in Drim?'

'Same as ever. A living grave with resident ghouls.'

'This TV thing should spice them up. Did you tell them they'd better cosy up to the minister and the village headmen?'

'Yes, that Fiona woman knew how to go about it.'

'I should think those silly village women will all be seeing themselves as film stars the minute they hear about it.'

'You know how they are up here, Hamish. They'll be split into two camps. There'll be those who are trying like mad to get their faces on the telly and the sour ones who stand around the location hoping to register their disapproval on camera.'

Hamish laughed. 'And no filming on the Sabbath.'

'I didn't tell them, and I'm not telling them until I've got the contract.'

* * *

43

Fiona lay on her bed in a room in the Tommel Castle Hotel and listened to the moaning of the wind outside. Thank God a location had been found! This series could make her name at last. If only she hadn't got to deal with Jamie. She felt uneasy about his work. She had read his 'bible', where he had set out plot, storyline, characters and casting.

If only it had been a regular TV detective series like Poirot or Miss Marple. Despite her acid remarks about the British viewing public, she knew the large viewing figures lay with Mr and Mrs Average. Ambition coursed through her veins. She would do her damned best to make it work.


A few rooms away, Sheila Burford was also awake. She had suggested to Fiona that they should phone up Patricia and invite her for dinner. Fiona had snorted and said the less they had to do with writers the better. Sheila felt guilty. She was sure there was going to be the most awful scene when Patricia found out what they were doing with her book.

She had not liked what she had seen of Drim. It was a grim place, and she guessed that was why the policeman had sent her there. Fiona had been right in the first place. There were plenty of pretty locations within easy reach of Glasgow. Her own role had moved from that of researcher to personal assistant to Fiona. For the first time in her young career, she began to wonder whether there might be life outside television, some sane sort of job. She had been with the television company for only two years and had never worked on a project as large as this one was going to be. It was amazing, too, that in cosy, overcrowded Britain there should be this vast, unpopulated landscape at the very north with its great acres of nothingness. She shivered despite the central heating.

Over in Drim, Miss Alice MacQueen, the local hairdresser, could not sleep for excitement. A television company was coming to film in Drim! They would have their own hairdresser, of course. Or would they? Business had been slack. The local women came in for a perm about every six months. But they would all be hoping to at least appear in a crowd scene, and they would all be wanting to get their hair done. A good bit of business and she could get a new kitchen unit from the DIY shop in Inverness. She finally drifted off to sleep and into a happy dream where she was no longer hairdressing in the front parlour of her cottage but had a posh salon with a smart staff in pink smocks.

Mrs Edie Aubrey, her neighbour, was also in a state of excitement. She had once run exercise classes in the community hall, but gradually the women had lost interest and Edie had felt time lying heavy on her hands. She would put up her poster on the notice board at the community hall in the morning. Perhaps she might get a part herself? Better get round to Alice in the morning and get her hair done.


Patricia Martyn-Broyd was awakened with the sound of the telephone ringing. She struggled out of bed. After midnight! Who could it be?

She picked up the receiver and gave a cautious, 'Yes?'

'I'm so sorry to ring so late. This is Mrs Struthers.'

The Cnothan minister's wife. 'What's the matter?'

'I've just heard that they're going to be filming your book in Drim!'

'Drim. Where's that?'

'It's just the other side of Lochdubh. Didn't you know?'

'No,' said Patricia bleakly. If they had chosen Drim, then it meant they had been up in Sutherland and had not even bothered to call on her.

'They were over at Major Neal's today. They're going to use his castle – Castle Drim.'

'Today? Are they still here?'

'Yes, three of them. They're staying at the Tommel Castle Hotel.'

'Thank you, Mrs Struthers,' said Patricia. She would need to go over there in the morning, find out why they had not troubled to consult her. It was *her* book!

But when she called at the hotel at nine o'clock the following morning, it was to find her quarry had checked out. Patricia drove into Lochdubh and then followed the signposts to Drim, a village she had never visited.

She gritted her teeth as her car slid and skidded down the hillside to Drim. The sky was black and a few flakes of snow were beginning to fall.

She saw a large van with the legend 'Strathclyde Television' painted on its side parked by the loch and in front of the general store.

She pulled up beside it and went inside. Fiona, Sheila and Jamie were talking to the owner, Jock Kennedy. They were making arrangements to use the store for filming.

Patricia's voice cut across their conversation. 'Ahem,' she said, 'I am surprised you did not call on me first to consult me.'

They all swung around, Fiona quickly masking her dismay. 'Why, Patricia,' she said with a smile. 'We were just going to call on you when we finished here. This is Jamie Gallagher, our scriptwriter. Jamie, Miss Patricia Martyn-Broyd, the author.'

Sheila knew that Jamie had a blinding hangover and that Jamie despised Patricia's writing, so she was surprised when Jamie beamed at Patricia and said, 'It's an honour to meet you. Perhaps you'd like to come along with us until we fix up our business here and see how it all works, and then we can have a bite of lunch?'

Patricia melted. 'That would be very exciting,' she said.

'Fiona, I'll leave you to finalize the arrangements with Jock here,' said Jamie. 'A word with you outside, Sheila.'

He ushered Sheila outside. Then he turned and faced her. 'Don't let that old bat get wind of what's in the script,' he hissed. 'And get your arse over to the major's and tell him the same thing or he can kiss his castle goodbye.'

'She's bound to find out sooner or later,' said Sheila.

'Then let it be later. I've worked with these authors before, and they're a pain. They all ponce about as if they've written *War and Peace* instead of a piece of shite. She'll just have to lump it. There's nothing in her contract about her having any say in the script.'

But do they have to be so nice to her? thought Sheila as she drove off towards the castle. It's going to be a terrible blow when she finds Drim Castle is going to be featured as a hippie sixties commune.

48

The major was in his modest bungalow home. 'I moved in here two years ago and rented the castle,' he said after he had served Sheila a cup of coffee. 'It's a hell of a place to heat and get cleaned.'

Sheila told him the reason for her visit.

'Funnily enough, I was talking over just that with Hamish Macbeth, the policeman at Lochdubh, and he said something to the effect that it would be cruel to let the old girl know at this stage. Let her have her dream for a bit longer. She couldn't stop it if she knew, could she?'

'No, but she could go to the press, although that would not make much difference. They must be used to writers complaining about their work being mangled on television.'

'I'm feeling sorry for her. What kind of woman is she?'

'In her seventies, but very fit. Very vain, but a bit shaky underneath, if that makes sense. I think maybe she's a more powerful personality than Harry Frame – that's our executive producer – realizes.'

'Whereas you, so young and experienced, do?' The major's eyes twinkled.

Sheila laughed. 'I'm not so hardened as the rest of them, so I notice people as people and not as commodities.'

'There's a great deal of excitement in Drim over this.' The major suddenly frowned. 'I just hope it doesn't lead to trouble like the last time.'

'You mean Drim's been used by a television company before?'

'No, it wasn't that. I was away at the time, but there was a young Englishman came up here to live. Very handsome. Flirted with all the ladies and broke a lot of hearts. He was murdered by the minister's wife.'

'Gosh, I remember reading about that.'

'Poor Hamish Macbeth got into trouble over that. He shocked a confession out of the minister's wife by confronting her with a dead body, but it was the wrong body, a rare specimen of Pictish man, and Hamish had every historian and palaeontologist in the country down on him like a ton of bricks.'

'Hamish recommended Drim.'

'That's probably his Highland humour. Drim's a funny place.'

'How do you mean funny?'

'You've seen it. It's locked away from the world at the end of the loch. Don't get many outsiders. There was a lot of malice and spite over the Englishman. I hope the women competing for parts in the series don't get at each other's throats. Your genuine Highlander is not like the lowland or central Scot. Can have very black and bitter passions when roused. Another coffee?'

'I should be getting back.' Sheila looked wistfully at the blazing coal fire. 'Oh, well, yes. They can do without me. I'm pretty much a chauffeur this trip.'

'Snow's coming. Bad forecast. You'd better find somewhere to stay the night.'

When Sheila returned to Drim it was to find the other two at the manse. There was a new minister since the time of the murder, a taciturn little man, Mr Jessop, with a mousy wife.

When Sheila arrived, he was patiently explaining that any filming on a Sunday would not go down well with the villagers.

'That will be all right,' said Fiona quickly, noticing Jamie's suppressed anger. 'I'm sure we'll all be glad of a break. Is there anywhere around here to have lunch?' She felt cross and cold and edgy. The manse had a stone floor, and she was sure the permafrost was creeping up her legs. She longed for a cigarette, but the minister's wife had said she disapproved of smoking.

'There's nowhere here,' said the minister, 'but my wife and I were just about to have lunch. You are welcome to join us.'

'No, we'll go back to Lochdubh and get something there,' said Jamie. 'Care to join us, Patricia?'

'Thank you ... Jamie,' said Patricia, feeling quite elated with all this first-name camaraderie. 'So everything has been arranged in Drim?'

'It's a start,' said Fiona, 'that's all. I'll be back up with the production manager, accountant, lawyer and so on to get everything properly and legally agreed on.'

As they sat together having lunch in the Napoli in Lochdubh, Sheila, looking out of the window, saw white sheets of snow beginning to block out the view.

'I think we'd better get back to the Tommel Castle Hotel and find beds,' she suggested. 'We can't travel in this.'

Jamie finished his wine, wiped his mouth on his napkin and said evenly, 'If you don't mind, we will leave for Glasgow immediately.'

'I really do not think a young lady like Sheila should be driving in this weather, or anyone else, for that matter,' said Patricia. 'I, for one, will find accommodation at the hotel.'

Jamie smiled at her. 'Send us the bill. No, no, least we can do. Come along, Sheila.'

'She'll never make it,' said Fiona as she climbed into the van.

'It's Sheila's job to drive,' snarled Jamie.

So Sheila drove on up over the hills, peering desperately through the blizzard, swinging the wheel to counteract skids. They were up on the moors when the van gave a final wild skid and ploughed into a snowbank. In vain did Sheila try to reverse.

'You'd better get out and go and find some help,' said Jamie.

'No,' said Fiona flatly. 'No one's going anywhere. We'll need to sit here and hope to God someone finds us.'

Hamish decided to go to the Napoli that evening. The blizzard was still howling, and the police station felt cold and bleak.

In the heady days when Hamish Macbeth had been promoted to sergeant, Willie Lamont, who served him in the restaurant, had been his constable. But Hamish had been demoted over the mix-up of the bodies at Drim, and Willie had married the pretty relative of the restaurant owner and left the police force to join the business.

When Hamish had ordered his food, Willie leaned against the table and said, 'We had the fillum people in here.'

'Oh, aye,' said Hamish. 'I gather they're going to use Drim.'

'Just look at that snow!' said Willie, peering out the window. 'A wee lassie to have to drive in that.'

'What are you talking about, Willie?'

'I heard that writer woman from Cnothan saying as how they should get beds at the hotel, but the man said that the lassie wi' the blonde hair should get on the road.'

Hamish swore. 'Damn it. That's suicide. Keep my meal warm for me, Willie.'

He hurried back to the police station and called the mountain rescue service, saying finally, 'I don't think they could possibly have got far.'

'We can't do anything until daylight, but we'll have the chopper out at dawn.'

'I'd better see if I can find them myself,' said Hamish gloomily, forgetting about his dinner.

He took out a backpack, made a pot of coffee and filled a thermos flask with it. Then he cut some sandwiches and added them. He put on a ski suit and goggles, strapped on his snow-shoes and set out, cursing under his breath and damning all townees who wittered on about nature, as if nature were some cuddly Walt Disney animal and not a wild, unpredict-able force.

He gave up after two hours and headed back to Lochdubh. Like the mountain rescue ser-vice, he, too, would have to wait until dawn.

At four in the morning, the van engine rattled and died.

'Get out and open the hood and see what's up,' shouted Jamie.

But Sheila found they were now buried so deep in snow that she could not open the door. White-faced, Fiona said, 'We'll suffocate.'

Fiona and Sheila were in the front and Jamie behind them.

'I'd better see if I can get something to make

holes in the snow,' said Sheila. She scrambled over the seats and into the back of the van. To her delight she found a length of hollow steel tubing. What it was doing there, she had no idea.

'I'll open the window and push this through so we can get some air.' She handed the pipe to Fiona and then scrambled back. She rolled down the window and began to scrabble with her fingers at the solid wall of snow until she had made a tunnel. Then she took the pipe and thrust it into the tunnel and rammed it upwards. 'I'll need to draw it back in from time to time and make sure it isn't blocked,' she said.

'We have no heating,' wailed Fiona. 'We're all going to die. How could you have been so stupid, Jamie?'

'It's not me that's stupid,' yelled Jamie. 'It's all the fault of that stupid bitch, who doesn't know how to drive. When does it get light here?'

'About ten in the morning in winter. And we'll never live that long.'


But the sky was pearly grey at nine o'clock when Hamish Macbeth set out again into the bleak white world. The snow had stopped and everything was uncannily quiet, as if the whole of the Highlands had died and now lay wrapped in a white shroud.

He marched ahead on his snowshoes, out of Lochdubh and up to the moors, keeping to where he guessed the road was but looking always to right and left in case they had skidded off it.

Hamish suddenly thought of Patricia and her holiday in Greece. Somewhere in the world outside this bleak wilderness the sun was shining and people were lying on the beach. He wanted to get as far away as possible from Sutherland. His mind drew back from the sunshine of faraway places and settled on the thought of the film company. I'd like to get away before it happens, he thought. *What happens?* screamed his mind, but then his sharp eyes saw a little piece of pipe sticking up above a snowbank.

He tunnelled with his gloved hands into the snowbank, and then he saw the gleam of green metal. Found them, he thought with relief. Now let's hope they're alive. He heard the clatter of a helicopter in the distance.

He scraped away at the snow until he had the back window of the van clear. He peered in. Fiona, Sheila and Jamie all seemed to be huddled together for warmth on the backseat. He knocked on the glass, but the still figures did not stir.

He stood back and waved frantically to the approaching helicopter and then crouched down beside the snowbank made by the covered van to protect himself from the flying snow as the helicopter landed.

Sheila struggled awake as she heard the roar of the landing helicopter. 'Fiona!' she cried, shaking her companion. 'We're being rescued.'

They both tried to rouse Jamie, but he appeared to be unconscious.

Sheila was never to forget that moment after daylight appeared around the van and the door was wrenched open. She tumbled out into Hamish Macbeth's arms and burst into tears. 'I thought that bastard had killed us,' she sobbed. 'I'll never forgive him.'

'Aye, well, into the helicopter with you,' said Hamish. 'They'll take you all to hospital.'

The head of the mountain rescue team supervised the lifting of Jamie's unconscious body into the helicopter. 'This lot should be made to pay for all this expense,' he grumbled. 'What sort of fools drive in the Highlands in this weather?'

Hamish stood with his hands on his hips until the helicopter was only a little dot against the brightening sky.

A light breeze sprang up and caressed his cheek, a breeze coming from the west. Wind's shifted, he thought. Thaw coming. Floods and mud. What a country!

He made his way slowly back to Lochdubh. Smoke was rising from cottage chimneys.

The Currie sisters, Nessie and Jessie, middle-aged village spinsters, were outside their cottage, the pale sunlight flashing off their glasses.

'Just the man!' cried Jessie. 'Come and shovel this snow.'

'Away wi' you,' said Hamish. 'I've been up since dawn.'

He trudged past.

'Call yourself a public servant!' Jessie shouted after him.

'I call myself one verra tired policeman,' Hamish shouted back.

And an uneasy one, he thought. I hope this film company stays away. I've got a bad feeling about the whole damn thing.

# Chapter Three

*Do not adultery commit;*
*Advantage rarely comes of it:*
*Thou shalt not steal; an empty feat,*
*When it's so lucrative to cheat:*
*Bear not false witness; let the lie*
*Have time on its own wings to fly*
*Thou shalt not covet; but tradition*
*Approves all forms of competition.*
— Arthur Hugh Clough

Often one cannot look back on the best time in one's life with any pleasure if it ends badly. So it was with Patricia Martyn-Broyd in the months leading up to the first day of filming.

During the long winter months, a glow of fame had kept her exhilarated. Local papers had interviewed her and one national. She had given a talk to the Mothers' Union at the church in Cnothan on writing. And although she had not been able to start on a new book, there was always that little word 'yet' to comfort her. When all the excitement died down, she knew she could get to work again and the words would flow.

She arose early on the first day of filming and dressed carefully. The weather was fine, unusually fine for the Highlands of Scotland, with the moors and tarns of Sutherland stretched out benignly under a cloudless sky. She put on a Liberty print dress – good clothes lasted forever and did not date – and a black straw hat. Had the postman not decided to change his schedule and deliver the mail to Patricia's end of the village first, then her feeling of euphoria might have lasted longer, but a square buff envelope with her publishers' logo slid through the letter box.

She picked it up, sat down at the table and slit it open with an old silver paper knife which had belonged to her father.

She pulled out six glossy book jackets.

She stared down at them in shock. Certainly the old title was there – *The Case of the Rising Tides* – and her name in curly white letters, Patricia Martyn-Broyd. But on the front of the jacket was a photograph of Penelope Gates, a nude Penelope Gates. Her back was to the camera, but she was holding a magnifying glass and looking over one bare shoulder with a voluptuous smile. Larger than Patricia's byline was the legend 'Now a Major TV Series, Starring Penelope Gates as Lady Harriet'.

On the back of the jacket was more advertising for the TV series, along with Jamie

Gallagher's name as scriptwriter, Fiona King as producer, then a list of the cast.

Her hands trembled. What had gone wrong? She had seen such detective stories on the bookshop shelves but had never bought them, assuming that the writer was some hack who had written the books from television scripts rather than being an original writer.

Angry colour flooded her normally white face. A naked woman portrayed as her Lady Harriet – elegant, cool, clever Lady Harriet!

She went to the sideboard and took out a bottle of whisky which she had won in a church raffle the previous year, poured herself a glass and drank it down.

Then she phoned Pheasant Books in London and demanded to speak to her editor, Sue Percival, whom she considered much too young for the job.

'Hi, Patricia!' said Sue in that awful nasal accent of hers which always made Patricia shudder.

'I have just received the book jackets,' began Patricia.

'Great, aren't they?'

Patricia took a deep breath. 'They are *disgusting*. I am shocked. They must be changed immediately.'

'What's up with them? I think they're ace.'

'What has a naked actress to do with the character I created? And who is going to buy this? The covers make me look like some hack who has written up the book from the TV series.'

'Look here,' said Sue sharply, 'you want to sell your book, don't you?'

'Of course.'

'Well, the bookshops will take a good number if it's going to be on TV. Without that book jacket, we may get very low sales indeed. I am sorry you feel this way. We'll see what we can do when your next book is reprinted.'

The angry flush slowly died out of Patricia's cheeks.

'Are you there?' asked Sue.

'Yes, yes,' said Patricia in a mollified voice. 'You must understand I know little about marketing.'

'Leave it to us, Pat,' said Sue. 'You'll be a star.'

Patricia said goodbye and slowly replaced the receiver. *Another* book to be published. And what did it matter what they put on the cover? It was *her* work the public would be reading.

Josh Gates awoke around his usual time, eleven in the morning. He remembered that Penelope was due to start filming that day. He smiled. He felt unusually well. Penelope had begged him to slow down on his drinking, and he'd only had a couple of pints the evening before. He was pleased with Penelope. The money was good, and this detective series would make her name. No more would people think of her as some sort of trollop.

Josh had strangely old-fashioned ideas. Films on Sky and cable television channels were full of writhing, naked bodies, but he ignored all that. Penelope taking off her clothes for anyone but him reflected badly, he thought, on his masculinity.

He had given his promise that he would not appear on the location. Penelope had hugged him and said that it would spoil her acting.

He wondered idly how to spend his day. He decided to go down to John Smith's bookshop in St Vincent Street and find something to read.

He crawled out of bed and picked up the clothes he had discarded the night before and put them on.

The bookshop, as usual, was crowded. He thumbed his way through several paperbacks and then, on impulse, asked an assistant whether he could look at the catalogue of forthcoming books.

She handed him an autumn catalogue, and he thumbed down the index until he found Patricia Martyn-Broyd's name. He turned to the page indicated and found himself staring down at a full-page spread advertising *The Case of the Rising Tides*. The book jacket was there in all its glory. He glared at the naked photograph of his wife and let out a roar of

'Slut!' The bookshop assistants went calmly about their work. Any bookshop had its daily quota of nuts as far as they were concerned.

Sweating with fury, he went to the map section and jerked out a road atlas, blinking to clear his fury-filmed eyes until he located the village of Drim. Then he bought an ordnance survey map for the Sutherland area and strode out of the shop, taking great gulps of air.

'I'll kill her!' he yelled to an astonished passerby.

Two policemen strolling along St Vincent Street stopped for a moment and looked at the retreating figure of Josh.

'Nutter,' said one policeman laconically.

'I know that one,' said the other. 'Thon's Josh Gates, married to that actress. Probably drunk.'

'How do you know him?'

'Booked him for drunk and disorderly last year.'

'Who's he going to kill?'

'Only himself, the way that one goes on. Fancy a hot pie?'

Fiona sat in Drim Castle in her makeshift office, biting the end of a pencil. She was upset at the script for the first episode. But her protests had caused Jamie Gallagher to throw the scene of all time and threaten to get her sacked. 'Back off,' Harry Frame had told her.

'BBC Scotland want Jamie's work, and that's what they'll get.'

But Fiona felt her job was going to be little more than a gofer, as Jamie fretted about camera angles and lighting. He had quarrelled not only with her, but with the production manager, Hal Forsyth, and with the director, Giles Brown.

Jamie had also tried to get Sheila Burford fired after he had tried to get into her room at the hotel. Sheila had phoned reception, and a couple of burly gamekeepers from the Tommel Castle Hotel estate had forcibly removed Jamie from outside her door.

But Harry Frame refused to be moved on the subject of Sheila. 'That lassie has potential,' he said, meaning, thought Fiona bleakly, that he wanted to get into Sheila's knickers as well.

Despite the blazing sunshine outside, the inside of the castle was cold and dark.

She sighed and ran over the budget again. If only Jamie would get well and truly drunk and fall into a peat bog and disappear forever.


Hamish Macbeth, entering Drim Castle half an hour later, looked like a pointing gun dog, thought Sheila as she met him in the hall. His nose was in the air, and one leg was raised as he halted in midstride.

'What's that smell?' he asked.

'I can't smell anything,' said Sheila, blue eyes limpid with innocence. 'Oh, maybe it's the joss sticks. They're starting with the commune scene in the first shot.'

'That's pot,' said Hamish.

'Cannabis? Oh, I'm sure you are mistaken. We're all drunks here.'

Nose sniffing busily, Hamish moved forward.

'You're imagining things,' said Sheila as Hamish headed inexorably for Fiona's office. She raised her voice and shouted, 'You cannot possibly believe that any of us would smoke pot!'

Hamish opened the door of Fiona's office and went inside. The window was wide open.

'Why, it's Mr Macbeth from Lochdubh,' said Fiona. Hamish went to the window, which was on the ground floor. He leaned out and picked up a roach from the flower bed and then held it up before Fiona. 'Yours?'

'Look here, Constable,' said Fiona, 'I'm under a lot of stress. It's not cocaine. If you ask me, pot should be legalized. It's a harmless, recreational drug.'

'I picked the pieces o' a driver out from his car after it had gone over a cliff last year. He'd been smoking your recreational drug. I'm a policeman and it's not legal, Miss King.'

'Call me Fiona.'

'Whether it's Fiona or Miss King, you are breaking the law.'

Fiona saw her career falling in ruins before her eyes, and all because of one measly joint.

She reached for her handbag. 'Perhaps this matter can be sorted out amicably, Officer.'

'Don't even think of bribing me,' said Hamish. 'You're in bad enough trouble as it is.'

'I wasn't going to bribe you,' said Fiona, near to tears, although that had been her intention. 'I was just going to show you how little of the stuff I have.'

'Then show me.'

Fiona took out a packet and handed it over.

Hamish turned round and said to Sheila, 'Close the door.'

Sheila closed the door and came to stand behind Fiona.

'It's the people up here that could do with your money,' said Hamish. 'I have no wish to disrupt the film. I'm giving you a warning. Don't let me catch you or anyone else with this stuff again.' He put the packet in his pocket and threw the roach back out of the window.

Fiona sighed with relief after he had left. It was not as if she were addicted to the stuff. That was the great thing about pot. You could take it or leave it. Still, there was a little left in that roach. She climbed out of the window and began to look for it.

In her caravan, Penelope put on her costume for the opening shots and thanked her stars that Josh was safely in Glasgow. It consisted of a gauzy, near-transparent Indian gown under which she was to wear nothing. The first scene was to be shot with the members of Lady Harriet's commune on the shore of Loch Drim. Penelope had planned her future on the journey north. When the series was filmed and just about to be aired, she would take her final payments and put them in a new account in her name only. She would tell Josh that payments had been delayed to explain why the cheques did not appear in their remaining joint bank account. Then she would leave him and go to London, and with any luck he would drink himself to death before he found her.

A girl arrived to do her make-up, and then Sheila came to drive her down to the set. 'I wonder what the locals are going to think of that getup,' said Sheila, 'not to mention our famous author.'

'I won't have to cope with it,' said Penelope. 'That's Fiona's job.'


There was quite a large audience on the waterfront to watch the first day of filming. Dressed in sixties Beatles style, the hippies wandered about, smoking and chatting. 'What do you think of your leading man?' Sheila asked Penelope as they moved forward to join the others.

'He's all right,' said Penelope, who privately thought that Gervase Hart, who played the part of the chief inspector, was painfully like Josh in drunkenness and bad temper. But she had learned quickly in her career never to criticize any actor. 'He doesn't appear in this scene, so I won't be seeing him today.'

'Places,' called the director, Giles Brown, a thin, nervous man with a straggly beard.

Sheila helped Penelope out of her coat. There was a gasp from the assembled locals.

Her costume did not leave much to the imagination, thought Hamish as Penelope's voluptuous curves were revealed by the thin gown.

The cast had rehearsed their lines over and over again in a cold, grimy church hall in Glasgow. The Highland day was sunny and warm, and there was an air of gaiety about the cast.

Then a voice cried, 'Stop! This cannot go on!'

Everyone turned round. The little minister, Mr Jessop, was thrusting his way to the front of the crowd.

'That woman is nearly naked!' he shouted.

Fiona moved quickly forward. 'It's only a film, Mr Jessop,' she said placatingly.

The minister was red with anger. 'I will not have such goings-on in my parish.'

Then Hamish saw Patricia's car driving down the hill into Drim. More trouble, he thought.

Patricia got out of her car and edged her way to the front of the crowd, saying in her authoritative voice, 'I am the writer. Let me through.'

Then she stopped, aghast at the sight of the hippies and the nearly naked Penelope, and all the joy of getting yet another book back in print fled from her mind. 'What is this travesty?' she asked in a thin voice.

The minister swung round, sensing an ally. 'Just look at that woman,' he cried, pointing a shaking finger at Penelope.

Patricia looked and quickly averted her eyes.

'It's like this, Minister,' said Jamie Gallagher with a false smile and truculent eyes. 'Lady Harriet is head of this commune in the Highlands, and –'

'*My* Lady Harriet!' Patricia was now as white as she had been red a moment before. She had consoled herself on the road over with the thought that the naked Penelope Gates on the cover of her book had just been a publicity stunt. Had she not seen weird and wonderful covers on paperback editions of Dickens? But for this slut to play Lady Harriet, noble, gallant, intelligent Lady Harriet, was past bearing.

'I forbid it,' she said. 'There is nothing in my book about any hippie commune.'

'There's nothing in your book that's filmable,' said Jamie. 'Och, calm down, woman. It's just a bit of poetic licence.'

'I shall have it stopped!'

'You can't do anything about it,' said Jamie. 'You signed the contract.'

Patricia stared at Fiona. 'Is this true?'

'Well, yes.'

'And who is this man?' demanded Patricia, who had forgotten what Jamie looked like.

'This is Jamie Gallagher, our scriptwriter.'

'You are a charlatan,' said Patricia to Jamie. 'Why say you are going to film my book and then change the whole thing?'

'I am making it suitable for television,' said Jamie. 'Can someone get this woman off the set and keep her off?'

'You are not filming pornography in my parish,' howled the minister.

'I think we should all go to the castle and talk this through,' said Fiona.


'How are things going in there?' Hamish asked Major Neal.

'Stormy, I think. I'm sorry for Miss Martyn-Broyd. She seems to be in shock.'

'They seem quieter now,' said Hamish, cocking an ear in the direction of Fiona's office. 'I'm surprised to hear that BBC Scotland think so highly of Jamie. You wouldn't think he could write anything intelligent.'

'Oh, did you see *Football Fever*?'

'Who didn't?' replied Hamish. *Football Fever* had been a television documentary on the lives and passions of Scottish football fans. It had been witty, clever and fascinating and had sold all over the world.

'Well, that was Jamie's script.'

'You can't tell a book from its cover,' said Hamish sententiously.

'It'll probably look all slick and clever when we see the finished result.'

'You could be right,' said Hamish. 'Here they come.'

The minister emerged with Fiona, Giles Brown and the production manager, Hal Forsyth. They were all laughing and chatting.

'So that's all settled,' said Giles, clapping the minister on the back.

'Most generous of you,' said the minister.

Greased his palm, thought Hamish

Then came Jamie, who strode past without a word. Where's Patricia? wondered Hamish.

When they had all left, he found her sitting alone in Fiona's office, clutching a script.

She looked up and saw Hamish. Her eyes were bleak. 'I'll kill him before I let him get away with this.'

'Who?'

'Jamie Gallagher. I told him right in front of all of them. "I'll kill you."' She began to cry.

Hamish sat down next to her and put an arm around her shoulders. 'There now,' he said. 'Just think about your books.'

'I am thinking about them,' sobbed Patricia. 'Look at this!'

She unfastened the clasp of her large handbag and took out one of the book jackets.

'Oh, my,' said Hamish. 'The things they do. But I saw a paperback of Jane Austen's *Emma* and if you didn't know the work, you'd have thought it was porn. Before I came up to the castle, I saw some press down by the waterfront. Why don't you go and say your piece to them? It pays to advertise.'

Patricia dried her eyes and blew her nose. 'It's all a nightmare. I just want to forget about the whole thing. It's the end of a dream.'

'You'll have a whole new readership. It could be the start of the dream.'

'I don't want the sort of readers who will be attracted by that cover.' Patricia put the cover back in the handbag and closed it with a snap. 'What happened to the world?' she said, looking about her in a dazed way.

It's moved on and left you behind, thought Hamish, but he did not say so.

After he had said goodbye to Patricia, he went back to the waterfront. 'How did you square it with the minister?' he asked Fiona.

'Contribution to the church – and that.' She pointed at Penelope.

Penelope was in the same gown, but underneath she wore a long silk underdress.

'Cleaning up the act?'

'Oh, we'll have the saucy bits in a set where we can keep the public out,' said Fiona. 'Where's Patricia?'

'Gone home to have a good cry, I should think. Why the hell buy her book if you want to change it that much?'

'We wanted a Scottish location, and the plot isn't bad. She should be grateful and shut up.'

The locals were beginning to drift off. It was all very boring. There seemed to be so many takes, so many long pauses, so little action.

Hamish reluctantly decided to go back to the police station and see if he was wanted for any duties.

His uneasy feeling about the whole business was melting away under the sunlight. Patricia now knew the worst and would get over her shock.

He had feared that the arrival of the television company would start up jealousies and rivalries among the village women, but the locals now looked bored with the whole thing.


Above the general store in Drim, Ailsa Kennedy, wife of the proprietor, Jock, was studying her new hairstyle in the mirror and wondering if that cow Alice MacQueen had gone out of her way to sabotage her chances of appearing on television. Before she went to Alice's, her fiery red hair had been long, almost to her waist. Now it had been chopped off and framed her face in one of those old-fashioned sixties styles with flicked-up ends. Alice could only manage old-fashioned styles.

Ailsa scowled at her reflection. Her husband's face appeared in the mirror behind her.

'What have you done to your hair?'

'Got it cut,' said Ailsa.

'You look a fright. I thought you said you'd never go near Alice's. It's this stupid fillum, and you're to have nothing to do with it, lass. Did you see thon actress? Near naked, if the minister hadn't made her cover up.'

'Oh, go away,' snapped Ailsa. 'You give me a headache.'

Jamie Gallagher heard the beat of music from the community hall and strolled inside. Village women were performing aerobics under the direction of Edie Aubrey.

He stared at them for a long moment and then went out again to search for Fiona. 'You'll never believe it,' he said when he found her. 'There's a whole time warp o' women in the community hall. You've never seen so many sixties hairstyles.'

'I'll have a look,' said Fiona.

Ailsa Kennedy had just finished washing out the last of the offending hairstyle and was drying her hair into a smooth bob when she heard her latest friend, Holly Andrews, calling from the shop below. 'Are you up there, Ailsa?'

'Coming,' called Ailsa, brushing down her hair.

She clattered down the steps to the shop.

Holly was a tubby middle-aged woman who had moved to a little cottage in Drim after the death of her husband. She had lived before his death in a large house on the outskirts of Lairg and after his death had sold up. Her brown hair was done in the same hairstyle that Ailsa had just vigorously washed out.

'What have you done to your hair?' gasped Holly.

'What d'you think? I washed it out. I looked like an aging Beatles fan.'

'They want our hair like this,' shrieked Holly. 'It's so exciting. The film's set in the sixties, and Alice has turned us out in sixties hairstyles because that's as far as she ever got in hairstyling, and the film people are wild about it. We're all to be in crowd scenes.'

Ailsa clutched her now-smooth hair. 'What have I done?'

'Go round to Alice's and get her to do it again,' urged Holly.

Ten minutes later, Alice, with a superior smile on her face, whipped a smock around Ailsa. 'I knew what I was doing,' she said. 'I knew it was set in the sixties.'

Ailsa bit back an angry retort. 'Just get on with it,' she muttered.

* * *

Jimmy Macleod, a crofter, listened in horror as his wife, Nancy, teetering on high heels across the stone flags of the kitchen floor, announced that she had a part in the film.

'You're not consorting with naked women and that's that,' said Jimmy.

His wife looked at him contemptuously.

'I'll put a stop to it right now.' He seized his jacket from a peg by the door and strode out.

In her office in Drim Castle, Fiona looked up wearily as Jimmy Macleod was ushered in by Sheila. He was a small man with rounded shoulders, a wrinkled face and an odd crablike walk.

'Whit's this about putting my wife in a fillum?' demanded Jimmy.

Fiona smiled at him. She had already dealt with two other irate husbands and knew exactly what to do.

'Wait right here,' she commanded. She made her hands into a square and surveyed the now bewildered Jimmy through them. 'Perfect,' she said.

'What are ye talking about, woman?'

'You look the perfect Highlander to me,' said Fiona. 'A very good face for one of our crowd scenes.'

Jimmy looked at her, his mouth open and the anger dying out of his face. 'You will be paid, of course,' said Fiona. 'Yes, we need the nobility of your face. What about a dram, Mr . . .?'

'Macleod, Jimmy Macleod.' Jimmy scuttled forward and sat down. His heart was beating very hard. He had gone to as many movies as he could afford when he was a boy. He felt as if some fairy had waved a wand and transformed him into Robert Redford. Fiona poured him a generous measure of whisky.

'Here's to a successful show,' said Fiona.

'Aye,' said Jimmy, a smile cracking his walnut face. 'Here's tae the fillum business.'

'Film business,' said Fiona, 'of which you are now a member.'

And Jimmy thought his heart would burst with pride.

Jamie Gallagher was swollen up with vanity and whisky. He felt he could have turned out the whole television series on his own. Had he not told the director which camera angles should be used? But going over the day's rushes, Fiona had objected to several of his choices, although the final choice would lie with Harry Frame.

Jamie left the bar of the Tommel Castle Hotel and went up to his room, where he phoned Harry Frame.

'We've a good team up here, Harry,' he said. 'But there's one person I cannae get along with and that's Fiona. She'll have to be replaced.'

Harry's voice squawked objections at the other end. The publicity had gone out with

Fiona's name on it. Jamie finally threatened to pull out of the series, and Harry capitulated.

Fiona listened to Harry ten minutes later on her mobile phone. 'You can't do this to me, Harry,' she said.

'I'm afraid I have to, luv. I'll find something else for you.'

'I'll kill Jamie,' said Fiona.

'I'll come up myself tomorrow,' said Harry.

'What's the point?' Fiona snapped her mobile phone shut and stared coldly into space.

The following morning Patricia sat down to read her daily copy of the *Scotsman*. She felt calmer now. She would just stay away from the film location, wait until her book was published and then the reviewers would surely point out how superior it was to the television production. Then she came across an interview with Jamie Gallagher, famous scriptwriter of *Football Fever*. In the interview, Jamie described how he had created *The Case of the Rising Tides* and the character of Lady Harriet. There was no mention of Patricia or that the television series had been adapted from one of her books.

'I'll kill him,' hissed Patricia. Then she ripped the newspaper to shreds.

* * *

Angus Harris sat sadly in the Glasgow flat of his late friend, Stuart Campbell, sorting through his effects. Angus had been away in the States and had only just discovered that his friend had died of AIDS during his absence and had left him his flat and effects in his will.

Stuart had been a struggling writer. A trunk was full of manuscripts. Angus did not know what to do. Perhaps he should find some literary agent and send off all these manuscripts in the hope that at least one would get published. He pulled them out one by one, stopping when he came to one entitled *Football Fever*.

He slowly opened it. It was the script for a television documentary. He frowned. It had been shown in the States on PBS, but he was sure Stuart's name hadn't been on it. It had originally been produced by BBC Scotland.

And then he remembered seeing something about it in that day's *Scotsman*. He went and got the paper and came to the interview with Jamie Gallagher.

It all clicked into place in his mind as he read the interview with Jamie. Stuart had written to him, saying that a scriptwriter called Jamie Gallagher was running an evening class to teach writers how to prepare a script for television.

'The bugger must have stolen it,' said Angus.

He set out to investigate. He called at BBC Scotland, but they had never heard of Stuart.

He tried to find out names of any people who had attended Jamie's classes, which had been held in the basement of a church. But there were no records, and no one could remember anything.

Angus knew his own violent temper was his weakness. But the thought that poor Stuart had died and someone had used his script to get international fame and glory was past bearing. This Jamie Gallagher was in Drim.

He would drive up there and confront him.

Josh Gates, hungover, ate his bacon and eggs in a bed-and-breakfast outside Perth as he read the interview with Jamie. Here was the man who was behind making his wife flaunt herself on television.

'He'll have me to reckon with!' howled Josh.

The other diners averted their eyes. This must be the madman whose drunken retching had kept them awake during the night.

Fiona moved through the next day as if walking in a nightmare. She could hardly bear to look at Jamie and at the triumphant little smirk on his face.

Harry Frame arrived, having flown to Inverness early in the morning and taken a taxi up to Drim. Typical, thought Fiona. I have to watch out for every penny, and he spends about a hundred and fifty pounds on a cab fare.

'Hang on for another week and be sweet to Jamie,' urged Harry. 'It might blow over.'

'No scriptwriter should have this amount of power,' said Fiona.

'Well, he hasn't done anything since *Football Fever*, but everyone still talks about that.'

Fiona picked up a script. 'But *Football Fever* was clever and witty, and this is just crap.'

'Jamie knows what he's doing,' said Harry.

'Well, let's take this location of Drim for a start. *The Case of the Rising Tides*. It's on a sea loch, but the tides don't rise and fall the way they would do at the seaside. Also, the climax of the book is based on the flooding of the spring tide, and this is summer and the tide doesn't flood.'

'I thought we weren't going by the book,' said Harry. 'What is it, Sheila?'

'There's an Angus Harris here, breathing blood and fire,' said Sheila. 'He says his friend Stuart Campbell wrote the script for *Football Fever* and Jamie pinched it.'

'Show him in,' said Fiona quickly.

Angus Harris was a good-looking young man with blond hair and a tanned face.

'What's this all about?' asked Fiona.

'This!' Angus held out the script of *Football Fever* he had discovered. 'My friend Stuart Campbell died when I was in the States. He left me his flat and effects. I was going through his stuff and I found this. Now Stuart attended a scriptwriting class given by Jamie Gallagher, and as I remember, the people in this class submitted various scripts to Gallagher for his opinion. The bastard must have copied Stuart's script and, hearing he was dead, submitted it as his own.'

'Do you have any proof of this?'

'Not yet. But I'll get it. I'll go the newspapers with this. I'm sure someone who was in the same class will read it and come forward.'

'Get Jamie in here,' Harry ordered Sheila.

They waited in silence until Jamie came in. With a certain amount of relish, Fiona described the reason for Angus's visit.

Jamie went off into full rant. 'How dare you!' he gasped. 'That was my script and no one else's. I gave up that class because they were a bunch of losers. I was wasting my time and talent on a bunch of no-hopers and wannabes. Och, I remember this Stuart Campbell. Useless wee faggot.'

Angus punched him on the nose, and Jamie reeled back, blood streaming down his face. 'Get the police!' howled Jamie, and Fiona picked up the phone.


Hamish Macbeth, arriving half an hour later, listened carefully, trying to sort out accusations from the babble of voices that greeted him. Jamie's voice was loudest, 'I'm charging this bastard with assault!'

'Wait a bit,' said Hamish soothingly. 'Now Mr Harris, as far as I can make out, the situation is this. You found a script of *Football Fever* amongst your dead friend's effects and came to the conclusion that he had written it.'

'I know he wrote it,' said Angus. 'It was his style.'

'Charge him,' said Jamie.

'In a moment,' said Hamish mildly. 'We'll deal with this business o' the script first. I'll phone Glasgow police and we'll take the matter from there. It should be easy to find someone who was at that class.'

The anger drained out of Jamie. 'Let's just leave it. I'm sorry I called Stuart a faggot. I don't feel like wasting my time appearing in a sheriff's court. I've got work to do.'

'But I think the matter should be investigated,' said Fiona sweetly. 'Plagiarism is a serious business.'

'You bitch!' snarled Jamie. 'You've just got it in for me because you're out of a job.'

'Now I've met you,' said Angus to Jamie, 'I can't believe for a minute that you wrote anything as intelligent and amusing as *Football Fever*. You're a dead man.'

'I'll look into it,' said Hamish. 'Although I gather the provocation was great, Mr Harris, don't go around hitting people.' He turned to Harry Frame. 'I'll let you know what I find out.'

Over in Lochdubh, Dr Brodie received a distress call from the minister's wife at Cnothan. 'It's Miss Martyn-Broyd. She's wandering around shouting something about killing someone, and our Dr MacWhirter is on holiday.'

Dr Brodie drove over to Cnothan. The first person he saw in the bleak main street was Patricia, striding up and down, clenching and unclenching her fists.

The doctor got out of the car. 'Miss Martyn-Broyd? I'll just be getting you home.'

'Leave me alone,' grumbled Patricia.

'This is a disgraceful way for a lady to behave,' said Dr Brodie.

She looked at him in dazed surprise and then began to cry. 'Get in the car,' ordered the doctor.

He drove her back to her cottage. He had called there once before when the local doctor had been on holiday. Patricia had thought she was suffering from a heart attack, but Dr Brodie had diagnosed a bad case of indigestion.

'Sit down,' he ordered when they were in her cottage, 'and tell me from the beginning what's put you in this state.'

Patricia began to talk and talk. She showed him the book jacket. She told him about her horror at seeing Penelope Gates on the set and finished by wailing, 'I'll be a laughing stock. I'll kill that man Gallagher.'

'You'll only be a laughing stock if you march about Cnothan speaking to yourself,' complained Dr Brodie. He noticed that Patricia was calm and reasonable now.

'I'm sorry,' she said. 'I don't know what came over me.'

'Have you any friends up here?' asked Dr Brodie.

'I know people in the church.'

'I meant real friends. A shoulder to cry on.'

'There is no one here I can relate to,' said Patricia with simple snobbery. 'They are not of my class.'

'I would drop that old-fashioned attitude and get out and about a bit more or go somewhere where you think you'll be amongst your own kind. I'm not giving you a sedative. I don't believe in them. But if it all gets too much for you again, I want you to phone me or come to my surgery in Lochdubh and talk it over. There is nothing like talking in a situation like this.'

When Dr Brodie drove back into Lochdubh, he saw Hamish Macbeth strolling along the waterfront and hailed him.

'What's this I hear about Patricia going bonkers?' asked Hamish.

'News travels fast in the Highlands,' said the doctor. 'The poor woman had a brainstorm because of the savaging of her work.'

'I don't like this film business at all,' said Hamish. 'I want it to work for the people in Drim – they could do with the money – but there's a bad feeling about the whole thing. I found out that Fiona woman, the producer, got fired because of Jamie Gallagher, the script-writer, and now there's a young man from Glasgow who says that Jamie pinched his friend's script for *Football Fever* and used it as his own. There's already been violence. The young man, Angus Harris, punched Gallagher on the nose. Och, I'm worrying too much. Maybe it's chust the way TV people go on!'

# Chapter Four

*I passed through the lonely street. The wind*
*   did sing and blow.*
*I could hear the policeman's feet. Clapping to*
*   and fro.*

                    – William Makepeace Thackeray

Major Neal, with true Highland thrift, was eating his lunch at the television company's mobile restaurant set up in the forecourt of the castle. It was another sunny day, and everyone seemed in good spirits. A week had passed since all the fuss from Patricia and Angus Harris.

Fiona King came in and collected a plate of food and joined him. 'Everything all right?' asked the major.

'It's all going splendidly because Jamie's taken himself off somewhere,' said Fiona. 'Harry's furious because he wants some changes to the script and Jamie didn't say anything about leaving.'

'Anything to do with that chap who says his friend wrote the script of *Football Fever*?'

'Could be. I wish he would stay away forever. If I had my way, I'd have another scriptwriter brought in. His stuff's pretty lifeless. I don't like this commune business, although Harry's all for it. There's something so trite about it all. Have you seen *Ballykiss-angel* on television?'

'Yes.'

'Well, it's Celtic whimsy, Irish Celtic whimsy at that, but it's guaranteed to run forever. It's soothing, it's funny and it's nice.'

'I thought niceness wasn't your forte,' said the major, his eyes twinkling. 'I've heard some of your remarks about Sunday night viewers.'

'I've changed,' said Fiona. 'I want a success. Besides, there's something about it up here. The quality of life.'

'It's a sunny day,' said the major cautiously, 'and even Drim seems like a nice place. But there are a lot of passions and rivalries here. It can be a difficult place to live in, particularly during the long dark winter.'

Fiona shuddered. 'Don't remind me of the winter. I thought we were all going to die. Pity Jamie recovered from hypothermia. He'd been drinking a lot, and that put him in a worse state than Sheila or myself.'

'Have you heard any more from Miss Martyn-Broyd?'

'No, thank God. Writers are tiresome creatures.'

'I thought you'd been fired.'

Fiona sighed. 'This is supposed to be my last day.'

Harry Frame's large bulk darkened the doorway. 'We really need to find out where Jamie's gone and get him back,' he said. 'I've put Sheila on to it.'

The manager of the Tommel Castle Hotel was, at that moment, unlocking Jamie's door for Sheila. 'I just want to make sure he's packed up and gone,' said Sheila.

He swung open the door. 'Help yourself.'

Sheila walked in, wrinkling her nose at the smell of stale cigarette smoke and whisky. 'The maids haven't got to this one yet,' said Mr Johnson. 'I know it's late, but we're short staffed. I'll leave you to it. Leave the key at reception when you're finished.'

Sheila opened the wardrobe door. It contained six shirts, one suit, an anorak and a raincoat. At the foot of the wardrobe was a selection of boots and shoes.

She stood back. On the top of the wardrobe was Jamie's suitcase. Sheila went into the bathroom. A battered toothbrush and a mangled tube of toothpaste stood in a tumbler on the washbasin.

She turned and went back into the room and opened the drawer in the bedside table. She stared down at Jamie's car keys and driving licence.

Sheila sat down on the bed. Wherever Jamie was it must be near at hand. Probably getting drunk somewhere. Then she realized the bed she was sitting on had not been slept in, and the manager had said the maids had not yet been in to clean the room.

She thought Jamie was probably sulking over the charges of plagiarism – no, wait a minute, that had been Fiona's word for it. What Jamie was accused of was outright theft of the whole manuscript.

She decided to drive down to the police station and see that nice policeman. He would know bars in the area where Jamie might be found.

As she drove along the waterfront, she could not help contrasting this view of sunny Lochdubh with the bleak white hell it had all been in the winter. How strange it was up here and how little she or her friends in Glasgow knew of the far north of Scotland.

Roses were rioting round the blue lamp over the front door of the police station, and Hamish Macbeth was lying back in a deck chair in his front garden, his eyes closed and his face turned up to the sun.

Sheila gave an apologetic cough, and Hamish opened his eyes. 'I was just meditating,' he said defensively. 'Would you like a cup of coffee?'

Sheila accepted the offer, and he said, 'Sit yourself down. I'll get the coffee and another seat.'

She sat down in the deck chair. It was so peaceful here. From the schoolroom along the road she could hear the voices of children reciting the four times table, a boat chugged lazily somewhere out on the loch and two buzzards sailed up into the blue sky above her head.

Hamish carried a small table into the garden and a chair, which he set down next to her. Then he went back into the house and re-appeared a short time later with a tray of coffee cups and a plate of biscuits.

'Now,' he said comfortably, sitting down next to her, 'what's up?'

'I can't find Jamie.'

To Sheila's surprise, he looked worried. 'That's bad,' he said slowly. 'Have you checked his hotel room?'

'Yes, and all his stuff's still there, including his car keys and toothbrush. I'm supposed to find him, but I don't know where to start. He might be in some pub.'

'He wasn't in any of them at closing time last night,' said Hamish. 'I did my rounds. I take away the car keys of anyone who's too drunk to drive home. When did you last see him?'

'Early last evening. We were up on the mountain above Drim. A television series is filmed in different bits, not necessarily in sequence. We were filming the bit where Lady Harriet is being chased across the top of the mountain by the murderer. We had to do it when we could get the helicopter. It was a busy day. All the equipment had to be lifted up to the top of the mountain. Jamie was here, there and everywhere, shouting orders, insulting everyone. Did you find out whether he had stolen that script or not?'

'I've asked a friend at Strathclyde police to look into it. I haven't heard anything yet. Is that chap Angus Harris still about?'

'He hung about for a few days and then took himself off.'

'Did you see Jamie come down from the mountain?'

Sheila wrinkled her brow. 'I can't remember. We lesser mortals had to scramble back down the track . . . you know the one?'

'Steep, but an easy climb.'

'Yes, that one. I thought Jamie would probably get a lift down in the helicopter.'

'What was he wearing? Was he dressed for climbing?'

'Oh, thick boots, jeans, checked shirt and that donkey jacket of his because it was pretty cold up there despite the sunshine.'

'Finish your coffee,' said Hamish. 'I'm going in to change.'

Sheila sat in the sunshine, reluctant to believe that anything serious had happened to Jamie. Still, a village policeman, unused to major crime, probably had become a bit carried away by the presence of a television company.

Hamish reappeared wearing shirt, stout corduroy trousers, jacket and climbing boots and a rucksack.

'You go back to the set,' he said. 'I'll chust be checking those mountains.'

I wish I were looking for someone I liked, thought Hamish as he trudged up through the foothills behind Drim and stared at the towering mountain above. Behind him came Jock Kennedy, who had left his wife in charge of the store while he volunteered to show Hamish where they had been filming the day before.

'The silly cheil's probably lying dead drunk somewhere,' said Jock. 'This fillum business has got all the women running around and screeching like hens.'

'Were any of them up on the mountain?'

'No, they were used for a crowd scene earlier, and my Ailsa was making a fool of herself, simpering and twittering.'

They toiled on upwards, reaching a steep path which wound between two cliffs of rock. The noises of the village faded away, and all was silence except for the grating of their climbing boots on the rock and the panting of Jock, who was beginning to find the climb heavy going.

Hamish saw two threads of material caught in a gorse bush and pulled them off and put them in a cellophane packet.

After a long climb, they reached a sort of heathery plateau at the top.

Jock sat down suddenly and panted, 'This is where they were.'

'Have a rest,' said Hamish. 'I'll look around for a wee bit.'

Jock leaned back in the heather and closed his eyes. Hamish trudged along, picking up various discarded bits and pieces: a crumpled cigarette packet, an empty Coke can, cigarette ends, chocolate biscuit wrappers and paper cups. He put the debris in a plastic bag as he went along, finally putting the bag down on a rock and weighting it down with a stone.

He shielded his eyes. A buzzard sailed lazily on a thermal. Then he heard the harsh cry of a hooded crow and quickened his pace, heading towards the sound of the crow.

The plateau dipped down to a bleak expanse of scree.

There, lying face up in the heather on the scree with two crows pecking at his dead eyes, lay Jamie Gallagher.

Hamish slithered down towards the body, flapping his hands, feeling sick.

'Jock!' he called. 'Here! Over here!'

Soon Jock's burly figure appeared above him. 'Oh, my God,' said Jock. He turned away, and Hamish heard the sound of retching.

Hamish struggled with his rucksack and took out a mobile phone. He tried to call police headquarters in Strathbane but could not get through, as often happened with cheap mobile phones in the wilds of the Highlands.

'Jock!' shouted Hamish. 'I'll stay here with the body. My phone won't work. Get help. Call Strathbane!'

Ailsa Kennedy stood on the waterfront and trained a pair of powerful binoculars on the mountain, which soared above the village. 'I don't know if I can go with you to Strathbane this evening,' she said impatiently to Holly. 'Jock went up the mountain with that policeman from Lochdubh. You know his temper. If he comes back to an empty house and no tea, he'll be fit to be tied.'

'You let him bully you,' said Holly.

Ailsa tossed her red hair. 'Nobody bullies me. Wait a bit. He's coming.' Then she lowered the glasses. 'He's as white as a sheet and looks in a right state.'

'What was he up there for?' asked Holly.

'To look for that scriptwriter.'

'Something bad must have happened,' said Holly. 'Edie, Alice!' She hailed the two women. 'Something's happened to that scriptwriter.

Jock went up to look for him, and he's coming back looking frit.'

Edie and Alice hailed more people. The gossip spread up to Drim Castle, and when Jock came running into the village it was to find everyone waiting for him.

'He's dead!' shouted Jock. 'He's got no eyes. He's dead!'

Fiona turned away a little. Sheila heard her mutter, 'Thank God.'

'He can't be dead,' shouted Harry Frame. 'And what's this about no eyes?'

'Hamish says we're to call the police,' panted Jock, running into the shop. Everyone who could get through the door crowded in after him.

Jock phoned Strathbane police and then sat down on a chair behind the counter. He fished out a bottle of whisky from under the counter and took a strong pull from it.

'What's this about him having no eyes?' asked Harry, shouldering his way up to the counter.

Recovering from his shock and beginning to enjoy the drama, Jock gave them a gruesome picture of the dead body.

'He knew about this,' said Sheila to Fiona.

'Who? What?' demanded Fiona sharply.

'Hamish Macbeth, the policeman. I went to ask his help to suggest some bar Jamie might be found drunk in. He got very serious about it all and said he would set out for where we were filming yesterday right away. He knew something was probably wrong.'

Fiona turned white and fainted and had it not been for the press of people about her would have fallen to the floor of the shop.

Up on the mountain, Hamish Macbeth peered at the dead body of Jamie. He hoped against hope that the man had died of alcohol poisoning. He eased down the springy heather which was pillowing the dead head and drew back with a little exclamation of dismay. The back of the head was crushed. He longed to turn the body over and inspect it thoroughly but knew he should not touch it.

He sat back on his heels and looked around. If Jamie had been struck down with some sort of blunt instrument, struck down from behind, why had he fallen on his back? Perhaps the killer had turned him over to make sure he was really dead.

The trouble with heather was that there would be no footprints. And who could have done it? Where had Angus Harris been the night before? Or Fiona? Or Patricia?

It was ironic it should be such a perfect day. Tourists travelled up as far as Sutherland to admire the scenery, but often the mountains were shrouded in mist and the villages drenched and grey in lashing rain. It was a day for a holiday, for picnics, for lazing around, not for sitting on the top of the mountain with a dead man whose eyes had been pecked out by the crows.

Then he heard the distant wail of police sirens and the faraway clatter of a helicopter. The bane of his life, Detective Chief Inspector Blair of Strathbane, had been on holiday. With any luck he might still be away. But as a helicopter suddenly soared over the top of the mountain and began to descend on to the heathery plateau, Hamish saw Blair's fat and unlovely features peering down.

The helicopter landed, and Blair, with his sidekicks, Detectives Harry Macnab and Jimmy Anderson, scuttled forward from the helicopter under the slowly revolving blades. Behind them came the pathologist, Mr Sinclair, tall, thin and sour, as if years of viewing dead bodies had curdled his nature.

'Whit's all this?' shouted Blair above the dying noise of the helicopter engine.

'The dead man is Jamie Gallagher, scriptwriter for a detective television series which is being shot here by Strathclyde Television,' said Hamish. He described finding the body.

'Sadistic murder,' said Blair. 'Someone poked his eyes out.'

'Crows,' said Hamish. 'Crows got at the body.'

'So it might not be murder?'

'The back of his head is crushed.'

'Oh, aye, and how did you find that out and him lying on his back?'

'I did not touch the body. I pressed down the heather his head's lying on.'

Blair grunted. Another helicopter roared in to land and disgorged a forensic team.

A tent was being erected over the body. Blair, who had turned away, swung back. 'You'd best get back tae your village duties, Macbeth. There's enough o' us experts here.'

'There's a lot of suspects,' said Hamish sharply.

'Aye, well, list them when you're typing up your report. I'll send Jimmy Anderson along to see you later.'

Hamish went wearily off down the mountain just as another helicopter bearing Chief Superintendent Peter Daviot arrived on the scene. The cost of all these helicopters, thought Hamish. There would be cuts in everyone's expenses for the rest of the year.

Daviot strode up to Blair and listened to his account. 'Where's Macbeth?' he asked when Blair had finished.

'He's got duties tae attend to and we don't need him here.'

'Does he know of any suspects?'

'Aye, he did say something about that.'

'Good heavens, man, he probably has a damn good idea who did it. I have often thought, Blair, that you let your jealousy of

that village bobby get in the way of an investigation. I'll see Macbeth myself.'

Daviot strode back to his helicopter. Blair
swore under his breath. He hoped Hamish
Macbeth had nothing to say but a load of
Highland rubbish.

Hamish reached the police station to find
Daviot waiting for him.

'Let's go inside,' said Daviot, 'and let's hear
what you know.'

Hamish led him into the police office, wiping dust from the desk with his sleeve.

'Now, let's begin at the beginning. Who
wanted this man dead?'

So Hamish outlined what had happened,
starting with his own recommendation of Drim.

'Why Drim?' interrupted the superintendent. 'It's a difficult place to get to and not the
prettiest around.'

Hamish gave him a limpid look. 'When I
heard it was a detective series, I thought they
might want somewhere a bit stark.'

He then described Patricia Martyn-Broyd's
distress at the savaging of her work, Fiona's
sacking and Angus Harris's accusation that
Jamie had stolen his friend's script. He finished by saying, 'Jamie Gallagher was a nasty
sort of drunk. He seemed to go around annoy-
ing everyone.'

'Was anyone actually heard to threaten
Jamie's life?'

'Well, the writer woman, for one,' said Hamish reluctantly.

'We'd better get her in. Type up your report. And try to work with Blair.'

'I try, I try –' Hamish sighed – 'but he doesnae seem to want to work with me.'

'He's a good man and a hard worker.'

When he's not drunk, thought Hamish.

'I know he's a bit jealous of you. Heard from Miss Halburton-Smythe?'

Hamish flushed. He had once been engaged to Priscilla Halburton-Smythe, a fact which had put him in high favour with Daviot, particularly Mrs Daviot, who was a dreadful snob.

'Priscilla's down in London,' said Hamish.

'Not helping her father run the Tommel Castle Hotel any more?'

'There was no call for it, sir. The manager does an excellent job.'

Daviot gave a little laugh. 'It's a pity that didn't work out for you. Mrs Daviot was most disappointed. But then, one cannot imagine Priscilla Halburton-Smythe as the wife of a village policeman.'

'Quite,' said Hamish, trying to block out a bright image of Priscilla with her calm features and smooth blonde hair.

'Anyway, type up your report. Blair will be with you later.'

The phone rang shrilly. Hamish picked it up. Blair's truculent voice asked for Daviot, and Hamish passed the receiver over.

Daviot listened and then gave an exclamation and said, 'That's great. Good work. It looks as if we've got our man. We'll have this wrapped up today.'

Daviot rang off. 'Blair's had a call from the police in Glasgow. Two policemen heard Josh Gates, the husband of Penelope Gates, who stars in the series, shouting in the middle of St Vincent Street, "I'll kill him." It turns out he was well-known in the business for blowing his top over his wife's various sexy roles. He'd been in Smith's bookshop and asked to see the catalogue of forthcoming books. Then he shouted, "Slut," and bought an ordnance survey map of this section of Sutherland. The bookseller's assistant said the catalogue was left open at a book illustration of *The Case of the Rising Tides*, showing his wife naked on the cover. We'll find him.'

Hamish typed up his report, feeling irritated and isolated. He itched to know what was going on. Had Josh Gates really committed the murder? If he had, he was probably in hiding somewhere.

He wondered if Patricia had heard the news. Surely she was bound to have heard about the murder by now. And where was Angus Harris?

It was eight o'clock in the evening by the

time Jimmy Anderson called. His long nose was red with sunburn.

'Filed your report?' asked Jimmy, sitting down wearily.

'Sent it to Strathbane ages ago,' said Hamish. 'The wonder o' computers.'

'Well, this case is nicely wrapped up. Got a dram?'

They were in the kitchen. Hamish went to the cupboard and brought down a bottle of cheap whisky. He knew Jimmy of old and was not going to waste good malt on him. 'So was it Josh Gates after all?'

'Yes, it was him.'

'Confessed?'

'No, dead as a doornail when they got him.'

'So how do they know he did it? What did he die of?'

'We're waiting for the pathology report, but it looks as if he got drunk and choked on his own vomit. He was lying up on the hill a little bit beside the road outside Drim. One of the locals found him.'

'So how do they know it was him?' asked Hamish impatiently.

'He had blood on his hands. They'll need to check the DNA. But we're pretty sure it'll turn out to be Jamie's blood.'

'What's the wife saying to this?'

'She says he had a violent temper and that after the series was over, she was going to leave him.'

'It's all too convenient,' muttered Hamish. 'What happens now with the TV series? Cancelled?'

'No, I gather Harry Frame considers it all wonderful publicity. They're all returning briefly to Glasgow to recoup, get another scriptwriter.'

'Why another? Hadn't Jamie written all the scripts?'

'He'd written the first two and the bible – that's the casting, story line, setting, all that – but they'll need someone or several to work out the remaining scripts, or maybe change the first ones. That Fiona King says Jamie's work was crap.'

'So she's still got her job?'

'Didn't know she had been fired.'

'Aye, Jamie got her fired. An ambitious woman, I think.'

'Och, we don't need to worry about her or anyone else. Thank God it's all tied up. Thon place, Drim, gies me the creeps.'

Hamish looked at him thoughtfully. He had an uneasy feeling it was all too pat. Yet Josh had been found dead with blood on his hands. But why should he have blood on his hands? If he had struck Jamie on the back of the head with a rock or a bottle or anything else and he were close enough, blood might have spurted on his clothes, but not his hands.

'Just supposing,' said Hamish slowly, 'Josh came across Jamie's body when the man was already dead. You'd think with that wound in the back of the head that he would be lying facedown in the heather. Josh wants to make sure he's dead, so he turns him over on his back and that's how he got the blood on his hands.'

'Who cares?' Jimmy finished his whisky and put the glass down and rose to his feet. 'It's all over.'


Soon Drim was emptied of television crew and actors and press. As if to mark their departure, the weather changed and a warm gust of wind blew rain in from the Atlantic and up the long sea loch of Drim. The tops of the mountains were shrouded in mist. Damp penetrated everything, and tempers in the village were frayed.

Excitement and glamour had gone. Only two determined women attended Edie's exercise class, and Alice's front parlour, which she used as a hair salon, stood empty.

Mr Jessop, the minister, thought he should feel glad that the 'foreign invasion' had left, but he felt uneasy. Everyone seemed to be squabbling and discontented.

He felt his wife was not much help in running the parish. Eileen Jessop, a small, faded woman, never interested herself in village affairs. It was her Christian duty, he thought sternly as he watched her knitting something lumpy in magenta wool, to do something to give the women of the village an interest.

'What can I do?' asked Eileen, blinking at him myopically in the dim light of the manse living room. Mr Jessop insisted she put only 40-watt bulbs in the light sockets to save money.

'You could organize some activity for them,' said the minister crossly. 'Weaving or something.'

'Why would they want to weave anything?' asked Eileen. 'The women buy their clothes from Marks and Spencer. And I don't know how to weave.'

'Think of something. You never talk to any of the women except to say good morning and good evening. Get to know them.'

Eileen stifled a sigh. 'I'll see what I can do.'


It started more as a venture to keep her husband quiet. The next day Eileen plucked up her courage and went down to the general store, where Ailsa was leaning on the counter and filing her nails.

'What can I do for you, Mrs Jessop?' asked Ailsa.

'I was wondering whether I could organize anything for the village women,' said Eileen timidly. 'Perhaps Scottish country dancing, something like that.'

'We all know fine how to dance,' said Ailsa.

She gave a rueful laugh. 'They were all hoping for parts in the fillum, that they were, and now they all feel flat.'

And then Eileen found herself saying, 'It's a pity we couldn't make a film of our own.'

'A grand idea, Mrs Jessop, but –'

'Eileen.'

'Eileen, then. A grand idea, but what do any of us know about filming?'

'My husband has a camcorder,' said Eileen, 'and I could get some books and maybe write a script. I was in my university dramatic society, and I wrote a couple of Scottish plays.'

Ailsa looked in surprise at the minister's wife, at her grey hair and glasses and at the jumble of shapeless clothes she wore. 'Funny,' she said, 'I cannae imagine you being in any amateur dramatic society.'

'That was before I married Mr Jessop, of course,' said Eileen, thinking treacherously of how marriage to a bad-tempered and domineering man had crushed the life out of her over the years. 'What do you say, Ailsa? Mr Jessop is going to Inverness this evening. We could have a meeting in the manse if you could round up some people who might be interested. There are some crowd scenes in the play. We could end up using everyone in the village.'

Ailsa suddenly smiled, and her blue eyes sparkled. 'You know, that would be the grand thing. What time?'

'Seven o'clock?'

'Fine, I'll see you then.'


Mr Jessop looked amazed and then gratified when his wife told him she was going to make an amateur film using the people of the village as actors.

'I'm glad to see you are taking your parish duties seriously at last,' he said waspishly. He never believed in praising anyone. It caused vanity.


A few weeks after the murder, Hamish Macbeth suddenly decided to call on Patricia. He put on the suit she had admired, Savile Row, bought from a thrift shop in Strathbane, and drove over to Cnothan and up to Patricia's cottage.

A light was shining in her living room, and as he approached the low door of her cottage, he could hear the busy clatter of the typewriter.

He knocked on the door and waited. At last, Patricia opened the door.

'Yes?' she demanded.

'Just a social call,' said Hamish.

'Come in, but not for long. I am writing.' She led him into the living room and sat down again behind the typewriter and looked at him enquiringly.

110

'I wondered how you were getting on,' said Hamish.

'Fine,' retorted Patricia, her fingers hovering impatiently over the keys.

'I gather from Major Neal that they're getting another scriptwriter and going ahead with the series.'

'It is no longer of any interest to me,' said Patricia. 'As you see, I am writing again, and that is more important than anything.'

Hamish leaned back in his chair and surveyed her. 'And yet you got a good bit of publicity out of the murder. I saw you interviewed on television several times.'

'I thought I came over very well,' said Patricia complacently.

Hamish privately thought Patricia had come over as cold and snobbish and patronizing.

'So what are you writing?' he asked.

'I don't want to talk about it until it's finished. I feel it's bad luck to talk about it.'

'Good luck to you anyway.'

'Thank you. Is there anything else?'

'No, no, just came for a chat.'

'Most kind of you, but I would really like to get on.'

Hamish left, feeling snubbed. He wondered why he had ever felt sorry for Patricia. The woman was as hard as nails!

Six scriptwriters were seated around the conference table at Strathclyde Television. The main scriptwriter was an Englishman, David Devery, thin, caustic and clever. Harry Frame did not like him but had to admit that he had put a lot of wit and humour into Jamie's scripts. The part of Lady Harriet had come to life. The commune had been written out. But Lady Harriet was to remain the blonde and voluptuous Penelope Gates, and she still seduced the chief inspector.

'We need to get all this rehearsed and get back up there as quickly as possible,' said Harry.

Sheila, filling cups over by the coffee machine, looked over her shoulder at Fiona. Fiona's normally hard-bitten face looked radiant. It was all going her way now, thought Sheila. With Jamie out of the way, the atmosphere of purpose and ambition had done wonders for Fiona.

And Jamie was more than dead. He was disgraced. Because of the publicity engendered by the murder, two people from Jamie's scriptwriting class had surfaced to say that Stuart had shown them that script of *Football Fever* and said he was going to give it to Jamie, that Jamie had cruelly trashed it, and Stuart had felt so low about it, he had said he would never write again.

Sheila found she was looking forward to going back to the Highlands. A picture of Hamish Macbeth rose in her mind. She wondered what he had really thought about

Jamie's murder. Penelope Gates, who had not seemed to mourn her husband one bit, had nonetheless told Sheila that she was puzzled by the murder. Josh, said Penelope, might have beaten her up, but murder Jamie? Never!

If Hamish were in a book like one of Patricia's, she thought dreamily, he would prove that Fiona had done it to keep her job. But Hamish was only the village bobby, and –

'What about that coffee, girl?' demanded Harry.

Sheila sighed. Harry called himself a feminist but never seemed to practice what he preached.

She put cups on a tray and carried them to the table. Her mind wandered back to the murder. BBC Scotland had agreed to pay royalties for *Football Fever* to Stuart's estate, which meant that Angus Harris had come into quite a bit of money. He had even sold several of Stuart's manuscripts to a publisher.

How neat it would be if Angus had done the murder. But no one had really been asked to produce an alibi. Josh had done it. Case closed.

# Chapter Five

*It almost makes me cry to tell*
*What foolish Harriet befell.*
— Heinrich Hoffman

Eileen Jessop watched the return of the television film crew with heavy eyes. Who would be interested in her amateur efforts now? It had all been going so well. The women had liked the Scottish comedy she had written so many years ago. She had felt important and popular for the first time in ages.

She wearily trudged down to the general store. Ailsa once more had her sixties hairstyle, and from the community hall came the *thump*, *thump*, *thump* of the music from Edie's exercise class.

'It's yourself, Eileen,' Ailsa hailed her. 'Going to get a part in the movies?'

Eileen shook her head.

'Och, you'll be following the camera crew around, getting tips.'

'I don't suppose any of the women will be interested in my little amateur venture any more,' said Eileen sadly.

'Don't say that! It's the best fun we've had in ages. I bet we could knock spots off this lot.'

Eileen blinked myopically. 'You mean you all want to go on?'

'Sure.' Ailsa leaned her freckled arms on the counter. 'See here, we always do our filming in the evening, and that's when this lot pack up. Of course we'll go on.'

Eileen gave her a blinding smile. 'That's wonderful. Mr Jessop doesn't mind the rehearsals and the filming at all.'

'Neither he should,' said Ailsa with a grin. 'We don't film on the Sabbath and there aren't any nude women in it.'

'I hope they all keep their clothes on in this television thing,' said Eileen anxiously. 'Mr Jessop's blood pressure is quite high.'

'Do you always call him Mr Jessop? Sounds like one o' thae Victorian novels.'

'I mean Colin. He likes me to call him Mr Jessop when talking about him.'

'Funny. But that's men for you.'


After the filming of *The Case of the Rising Tides* got well under way, Sheila Burford found herself increasingly reluctant to return to the Tommel Castle Hotel in the evenings with the rest of them to talk endless shop. She was becoming more and more disenchanted with the television world and was beginning to wonder if she had got into it because it made her mother so proud of her and all her friends seemed to think she had an exciting job. Sometimes she felt like some sort of maid, fetching and carrying and serving drinks and coffee.

After the first week, she drove to the police station.

'There's that blonde calling on Hamish Macbeth,' said Jessie Currie to her sister, Nessie. 'He can't keep his hands off them.'

Sheila, all too aware of two pairs of eyes scrutinizing her from behind thick glasses, knocked at the kitchen door of the police station.

'Come in,' said Hamish Macbeth cheerfully. 'Nothing wrong, is there?'

'No, I just got bored with television chatter.'

She followed him into the kitchen.

'Filming going all right?' asked Hamish.

'Oh, like clockwork, good script, everyone pulling together. It's as if Jamie had never existed.'

Hamish put a battered old kettle on top of the wood burning stove. 'It's a warm evening,' said Sheila, who was wearing a T-shirt with the Strathclyde Television logo and a pair of cut-off jeans and large boots. 'Do you always have that burning?'

'I was just about to put on my dinner. Want to join me? It's only chicken casserole.'

'If you're sure ... That would be nice.'

'All right. We'll have coffee first ... So Jamie's conveniently dead and everyone is happy. Fiona's kept her job and Angus Harris has come into money and Penelope Gates has lost a husband she didn't much like anyway. How's Penelope bearing up?'

'Remarkably well,' said Sheila drily. 'In fact, she's becoming a bit starry.'

'Meaning?'

'She's beginning to queen about a bit. It's odd, that. When Jamie was alive, she was very pleasant and subdued and only really came to life on the set. A hardworking actress, not all that great, but she has the looks. Now she seems to fly off the handle over every little thing and has to be coaxed back into a good temper.'

There was a silence while the kettle boiled. Hamish put instant coffee in two mugs and then carried them to the table and sat down next to Sheila.

'So were you surprised when you found out the murderer was Josh?' he asked.

Sheila took a sip of coffee and wrinkled her smooth brow. She was a very pretty girl, reflected Hamish, and almost immediately, Down, Hamish, you've had enough rejections to last you a lifetime!

'I was,' said Sheila. 'Just a feeling.'

'Why?' asked Hamish curiously.

'Well, the only proof it was Josh was the blood on his hands.'

'I thought of that,' said Hamish. 'He could have been skulking about up on the mountain and found Jamie dead. The body had been turned over.'

'Did they ever find out what struck him?'

'A rock. They found infinitesimal traces of rock in his skull. But all the murderer had to do was throw it away. Just below that bit of heather where he was lying is a whole expanse of scree. If the rock had been hurled down there, well, it could be anywhere.'

'Did they look?'

'Yes, they had a team o' coppers crawling over the mountain like ants.' Hamish suddenly froze, his mouth a little open.

'What's the matter?' asked Sheila sharply.

'I've chust remembered something,' he muttered. He could feel sweat trickling down from under his armpits. 'Excuse me,' he said.

He went through to the bathroom and stripped off his shirt and sponged himself down, then went through to the bedroom and put on a clean shirt. What sort of policeman was he? He had put all the bits and pieces he had picked up off the heather into his backpack and, after finding the body, had forgotten all about them. The plastic bag he had put them in and the cellophane packet with those two threads of cloth were still in the backpack, which he had thrown in the bottom of the wardrobe. When Jimmy had called to tell him that the case was all wrapped up, he had forgotten all about them. He should have handed them over to the forensic team when he left the mountain.

He returned to the kitchen. 'I'll chust put the casserole in the oven and we'll move to the living room. It's hot in here.'

Sheila looked curiously at him as she sat down in the living room. 'Are you sure you haven't had a shock?' she asked. 'Was it something I said?'

'No, no? I chust remembered I had a report to type up.'

'Am I holding you back?'

'Och, I can do it tomorrow.'

There was a knock at the kitchen door. Hamish went to answer it. The Currie sisters pushed past him and went straight through to the living room.

'We didn't know anyone was here, didn't know anyone was here,' said Jessie, who had an irritating habit of repeating everything. 'We dropped by to bring you a lettuce from the garden, the garden. And this is . . .?'

'Miss Sheila Burford, who is with the television company,' said Hamish. 'Sheila, the Misses Currie, Nessie and Jessie.'

'Pleased to meet you,' said Sheila, recognizing the two who had stared at her so fiercely on her arrival at the police station.

'Is there any trouble at Drim?' asked Nessie.

'Trouble at Drim,' echoed Jessie.

'No, this is just a social call.'

'Is there any news of Miss Halburton-Smythe coming up here soon?' asked Nessie.

'I have not heard from Miss Halburton-Smythe,' said Hamish stiffly.

'Such a beautiful girl,' said Nessie.

'Beautiful,' said Jessie.

'Was engaged to Hamish here, but he didnae appreciate her.'

'Appreciate her.'

'And went to foreign parts.'

'Foreign parts.'

'To hide a broken heart.'

'Broken heart.'

'Havers!' shouted Hamish, exasperated. 'I thank you kindly for the lettuce, but I am chust about to prepare dinner.'

'We're going, going,' said Jessie huffily.

Hamish ushered them out.

'Sorry about that,' he said.

Sheila grinned. 'Who is this Miss Halburton-Smythe? Anything to do with the Tommel Castle Hotel?'

'Her father owns it, we were engaged once, didn't work, end of story. I'll get the food.'

When they were seated in the kitchen with the stove now damped down and the door and window open to the evening air, Sheila said, 'It amazes me that it hardly ever gets dark up here.'

'The nights are beginning to draw in all the same,' said Hamish. 'In June it's light all night.'

'At least we'll be finished and out of here by the winter,' said Sheila with a reminiscent shiver.

'It wass unusual, all that snow,' said Hamish, but thinking uneasily instead of that plastic bag at the bottom of his wardrobe. His accent, as usual, increased in sibilancy when he was upset. 'To get back to Penelope Gates, she's employed by the television company. Why doesn't the director or whateffer chust tell her to do her job and cut the histrionics?'

'She's the star of the show, and stars, however small they might be, can rule the roost.'

'Is she on anything?' asked Hamish, remembering the pot-smoking Fiona. 'Uppers or anything?'

'No, I think she was kept down by Josh, and now he's gone, she's bursting out all over the place.'

'In every sense of the word, I suppose,' said Hamish. 'Unless the naughty scenes have been cut.'

'No, they're still in. She seduces the chief inspector tomorrow. They've built a bedroom set in the castle, four-poster and all that. But it'll be away from the eyes of the villagers.'

'A good thing, too,' said Hamish. 'The minister would have something to say about it.'

'I gather the minister's wife, Eileen, is making a film of her own.'

'That crushed wee woman! I don't believe it.'

'Fact. One of the village women told me. Eileen wrote a play when she was at university. They're performing that, and Eileen's filming it with her camcorder.'

'And what does the minister have to say?'

'He seems pleased. He doesn't like us TV people being back, but Fiona gave him a generous donation to the church. This chicken is very good. Just as a matter of interest, what's Patricia doing?'

'She's writing again.'

'Where was she on the day Jamie got killed?'

'Out walking, she says.'

'I had her down as the murderess,' said Sheila. 'She was so outraged. She's got a medieval kind of face. I could imagine her being quite ruthless.'

'If she was ruthless,' said Hamish, 'she would have found some hot-shot lawyer to try to break the terms of her contract.'

'You may be right.'

Hamish surveyed her. 'You definitely don't think Josh murdered Jamie.'

'I'm fantasizing,' said Sheila. 'Read too many detective stories. I suppose the police know what they're doing.'

Hamish said nothing, but he wondered whether Strathbane police, because of pressure from the media, had not jumped too thankfully to the easiest conclusion.

'I'm sorry I havenae any wine to go with the meal,' he said.

'That's why I'm here,' said Sheila. 'The dinners at the hotel get a bit boozy.'

'So tell me about yourself. How did you get into the television business?'

'I went to college in New York, in Washington Square in the Village, to learn all about filming. I did a short film and won the Helena Rubinstein prize. I was homesick, so as soon as I finished the course, I returned to Glasgow and applied for a job on Strathclyde Television. They said I should start at the bottom and learn the ropes. I've been there two years and I'm still at the bottom, fetching and carrying and making coffee, fixing hotels, driving that minibus around.'

'So why don't you try the BBC or ITV or maybe one of the cable channels?'

'Because I'm suddenly sick of the whole business. I think I might take a computing course. I'm interested in computer graphics.'

'All the beautiful girls end up studying computers,' said Hamish.

'Is that what took Miss Halburton-Smythe away?'

'Yes,' he said curtly. 'More coffee?'

Sheila wished she hadn't made that remark. There was a certain chill in the air which had nothing to do with the weather.

When she had finished her coffee, Hamish

said, 'Now if you don't mind, I'd better get on with that report.'

'Thanks for dinner. You must let me take you out.'

'Aye, that would be grand.'

'What about tomorrow?'

Hamish hesitated. 'Give me the number of your mobile and I'll phone you.'

Which you won't, thought Sheila sadly as she walked to her car.

When she had gone, Hamish went through to the bedroom, hauled out the backpack and took out the plastic bag and emptied the contents on the floor. Nothing much here, he thought with relief: old Coke cans, cigarette ends, a book of matches, but with no advertising on it, no sinister nightclub or sleazy bar such as they were always finding in detective novels. Then there was the little envelope with the two threads of cloth. Bluish tweed. What had Josh been wearing?

He should throw this lot away and forget about it.

Case closed.

Patricia Martyn-Broyd received a letter from her publishers. She weighed the large buff envelope in her hand and then slit it open. She pulled out book jackets and a letter from her editor, Sue Percival.

'Dear Patricia,' Sue had written. 'As you will see, we have changed the book jackets, feeling the original ones might not have been too tasteful in view of the murder. We hope you like them.'

The new cover showed Penelope Gates dressed in tweed hacking jacket, knee breeches, lovat stockings and brogues, standing on a heathery hillside, looking down at the village of Drim. Patricia's name was larger and more prominent this time.

She heaved a sigh of relief. Everything was working out quite well. Harry Frame had called to tell her they had cut out the commune scenes. She smiled.

It was time she visited the location and saw what they were doing. She was pleased with the new covers, *very* pleased.


'This coffee tastes like filth,' said Penelope Gates, throwing the contents against the wall of her caravan. 'Get me a decent one.'

'Get it yourself,' said Sheila. 'Who the hell do you think you are? You've started to behave like a maniac.'

Penelope looked at her with narrowed eyes. 'You have just got yourself out of a job, Sheila. I'll speak to Harry Frame today.'

Sheila opened the door of the caravan and walked out. Then she shouted through the open door, 'I hope you break your bloody neck!'

'Here, what's all this about?' demanded the director, Giles Brown, coming up to her.

'It's that bitch,' said Sheila. 'I can't take any more of her prima donna tantrums.'

'You'll just have to put up with it,' said Giles. 'We have to keep her in a good mood. We can't get anyone else at this late date. We've already lost a lot of money over Jamie's death. Think of all the publicity we've put out about Penelope. I know, I know, we're all beginning to realize why her husband beat her. I'll have a word with her.'

He went into the caravan. Penelope surveyed him with baleful blue eyes. 'I want that bitch fired,' she said.

'I'll see about it,' said Giles wearily. 'Look, luv, it's all been going well. Don't we all run around and look after you?'

'Let me know when you've fired her,' said Penelope coldly. 'You want this sex scene to work, don't you? Well, just see that no one else upsets me and get me a decent cup of coffee.'

'Sure, Penelope. Anything you say.'

Penelope smiled to herself. She took out a packet of amphetamines and swallowed two. They would give her the necessary buzz she needed for the filming. It had been wonderful since Josh died. She had been bullied by her parents, bullied by schoolteachers and bullied

127

by Josh. She hardly ever saw her parents now and Josh was dead and she was her own woman and free to take revenge on every bastard who tried to push her around. She had been feeling very exhausted since Josh's death, what with the shock of it all, and a friend had introduced her to 'uppers'. Penelope felt strong and in command of every situation for the first time in her life.

'No funny business now,' said Giles Brown to Gervase Hart, the leading man, or rather the anti-leading man, in that he was playing the part of the brutish chief inspector. 'You're only playing a sex scene, not performing it. I'm having trouble enough with Penelope as it is. I don't want her screaming rape.'

'I couldn't get it up for that nasty creature who thinks she's God's gift,' sneered Gervase.

'You won't be shot too explicitly,' said Giles. 'Bit like *Four Weddings and a Funeral*. Bits of flesh and a shoulder strap sort of thing.'

Gervase was a heavyset man whose once good-looking face had become a trifle spongy with drink, the features blurred as if someone had passed a sponge over them. Despite his bouts of drinking, he was a competent actor and never late on the set.

'What happened to Penelope?' he asked. 'I mean, when we started up here, she was a delight to work with. Now she bitches and complains about everything.'

'I think her husband's murder shook her more than we can know,' said Giles, ever placating.

'Maybe she did it.'

'No, he choked to death on his own vomit. No doubt about that.'

'Look, Giles, take her out to dinner and have a long talk with her. Soothe her down. We're all getting on so well. She's been all right, but her bad behaviour seems to have accelerated in the last few days.'

'I'll try,' sighed Giles. 'You didn't let slip to any of the villagers about this sex scene?'

'Close as a clam, that's me,' said Gervase shiftily, because he could not quite remember anything he had said the evening before.


On her way to Drim, Patricia stopped her car in Lochdubh and went into Patel's general store to buy some groceries. Patel had a better selection than the shop in Cnothan. There were various other customers, and Patricia was, as usual, a bit disappointed that no one came up and asked for her autograph or said, 'I saw you on television.' The fact was that most of Lochdubh *had* seen her being interviewed on television and had not liked what they had seen at all and were damned if they were going to give her any recognition.

Patricia was, however, particularly gracious to Mr Patel because he was an Indian. Patricia, who still mourned the loss of the British Empire, thought that all those poor Indians had been thrown into a sort of outer darkness by getting their independence and it was no wonder that Mr Patel had fled to Scotland.

She meant to be gracious but came across as patronizing, and Mr Patel was quite curt.

She went out into the hazy sunlight. She looked up at the sky. Long streamers of clouds were trailing across the blue, heralding a change of weather. The midges, those irritating Scottish mosquitoes, had reappeared, and she fished a stick of repellent out of her capacious handbag and rubbed her face.

'Mrs Martyn-Broyd?' A large tweedy woman was hailing her, hand outstretched.

'I am Mrs Wellington, wife of the minister here,' she said.

Patricia murmured something and held out her own hand and found it being pumped energetically.

'We have not been introduced,' said Mrs Wellington, 'but I had to speak to you. I am surprised that you should condone such behaviour.'

'What are you talking about?' asked Patricia, stepping back because Mrs Wellington had a way of thrusting her bosom forward to the person she was addressing and standing very close up.

'This television thing *is* based on your books, is it not?'

'Yes.'

'I cannot understand why a lady like yourself can condone sexual intercourse appearing on television.'

'What?'

'Sexual intercourse.' Several fishermen stopped their promenade along the waterfront to listen in amusement to the minister's wife.

Two spots of colour burned on Patricia's white cheeks. 'Explain yourself,' she snapped.

'Some actor was drinking in the hotel bar last night and he was heard to say, "I'll be screwing Penelope Gates tomorrow." He was asked about it, and he said he and Penelope were to be filmed in bed together in a set in Drim Castle *and without a stitch on.*'

'This shall be stopped,' panted Patricia. 'I won't allow it.'

'Good,' said Mrs Wellington approvingly. 'I myself will phone the minister in Drim.'

Patricia strode off to her car, her brain in a turmoil of rage and anxiety.

'Where are you going?' barked Mr Jessop as Eileen was heading out the door, her camcorder in one hand.

Eileen stopped and blinked at him myopically. 'I am going to see one of those TV

131

cameramen. He said he could give me a few pointers.'

'You are to go nowhere near any of them.'

'Why?'

'Do as you're told, woman. I'm off to the castle to deal with something.'

'Now, Gervase,' Giles Brown was saying, 'you come into the bedroom, you see her naked on the bed, smiling at you, and you start to tear off your uniform. Your eyes gleam with lust.'

'Sure,' said Gervase in a bored voice.

'Let's just run through it first,' said Giles.

Penelope appeared from behind a screen. She was stark naked.

Definitely a 38D cup, thought Fiona. What a figure!

Penelope lay down on the bed. She raised herself on one elbow and smiled seductively at Gervase, who began to tear off his clothes. When he was naked, he approached the bed.

Penelope rolled on her back and laughed uproariously.

'What's up?' asked Fiona crossly.

'Him!' said Penelope when she could. 'Have you ever seen such an ugly body? Jesus wept, he's got breasts like a woman.'

Before anyone could say anything, the door of the room opened and Mr Jessop, followed by Patricia, burst in.

'What is going on here?' shouted the minister.

'How dare you turn my work into pornography!' screamed Patricia.

Fiona saw disaster and moved quickly. 'Come outside and I'll explain things. We were just rehearsing until their costumes arrived.'

She shooed them out of the room and led them along to her office.

'It's like this,' she lied. 'Actors are used to seeing each other naked. No one thinks anything of it. They'll be dressed in the actual scene. Penelope will be wearing a nightdress and Gervase pyjamas.'

'I do not believe you,' said Patricia.

'Wait a minute and I'll arrange for them to show you the actual scene.'

Fiona sped back to the set and said to Giles, 'Get them both into nightclothes, and you two, perform a decorous petting scene. Sheila, get a nightgown and pyjamas fast.'

She then went back to the office. 'You can see the scene in a few moments.'

'This is a trick,' said Mr Jessop. 'There was some actor telling the locals last night how he was going to have intercourse with that actress.'

'Now, Mr Jessop,' cooed Fiona, 'do you think we would show such a scene? Gervase must have been a bit drunk, and he brags a lot. This is for family viewing. Nudity may be shocking to you, but we're used to it. I mean, have you seen some of the beaches in Spain, or even

Brighton? Nobody thinks anything these days about going naked.'

'You must think us very silly to be taken in by such a story,' said Patricia.

Fiona forced herself to smile calmly. All would be well just so long as this precious pair did not ask for any confirmation in writing.

'Television is a mad world.' She spread her hands ruefully. 'But just think. Would we jeopardize our chances of getting the prime family slot on Sunday viewing by showing explicit sex scenes?'

Sheila put her head round the door. 'Ready for you.'

'Come along,' said Fiona, 'and you'll see for yourselves.'

Penelope and Gervase, alarmed into good behaviour by the threat that the series might be sabotaged, were now dressed: Penelope in a long Laura Ashley cotton nightgown and Gervase in striped pyjamas rather like the minister's own. Fiona thought the wretched pair were deliberately hamming it up to make it look and sound like a Victorian courting scene. Certainly they ended up in bed together, but they finished the scene with a chaste kiss.

'And we fade there,' said Fiona brightly.

But old-fashioned Patricia and Mr Jessop had found it all very tasteful. They did not know that Penelope and Gervase had made up the lines as they went along.

'But they are not married and they are in bed together,' said Mr Jessop cautiously.

Fiona seized a script and pretended to consult it. 'A gamekeeper bursts in at that moment and says, "There's a body on the beach." They both hurry off to investigate. Nothing further happens between them.'

Relieved, Patricia and the minister accepted this explanation. They could not believe that these television people would go to such lengths to deceive them. Fiona took them back to the office, served them coffee and talked soothingly and flatteringly about the genius of Patricia's writing.

Patricia left, feeling quite elated.

Having seen them off the premises and having instructed two men to guard the door of the set in future, Fiona went back into the 'bedroom'. Giles was sitting in a corner, clutching his head.

'What the fuck's up now?' asked Fiona, her temper breaking.

'That bitch,' said Gervase, pointing a shaking finger at Penelope.

'She won't stop laughing,' mourned Giles.

'You cannot expect me to seriously make love to a man with a body like that,' sneered Penelope.

'Look here,' said Fiona wrathfully, advancing on Penelope. 'If you do not do what you are paid to do and keep making trouble, we'll find someone else.'

'You can't afford to,' said Penelope, looking at her with dislike. 'I hate being pushed around by people. I've been pushed around all my life, and I'm not going to take any more of it. Get rid of me? It'd be cheaper to get rid of *you*. Harry Frame'll be here later. Let's see what he has to say about it.'

Fiona tried to laugh it all off. It certainly would be easier to get rid of her than Penelope. 'Come on, Penelope,' she coaxed. 'Let's just get the scene done.'

'I've a headache now,' said Penelope mulishly. 'Tell Harry to come and see me when he arrives.'

She swept out.

'She's costing us money,' said Hal Forsyth, the production manager. 'Who does she think she is? Liz Taylor?'

'Tell Harry to see me before he sees her,' said Fiona.

Sheila followed her out. 'I want a word with you, Fiona.'

'Not you, too.'

'I've got something to tell you which might help. I was down in Lochdubh visiting that policeman. He said something about Penelope being on uppers, and I said then I didn't think so, but now I'm beginning to wonder.'

Fiona swung round. 'You mean, find proof and get her arrested?'

'I think Hamish would just give her a warning. No, I was thinking, she'll leave her caravan for lunch. I could go in there, search around, and if I find them, confiscate the lot. I think that's maybe what's been turning her into an aggressive bitch. It's worth a try.'

'Do it.'

Sheila hung around Penelope's trailer until she saw her stepping down and making her way to the temporary restaurant.

She had a spare key. She let herself in. Penelope's handbag was lying on the dressing table. She went through the contents until she came upon two bottles of pills. One was marked Librium and had a chemist's name on it. The other bottle did not carry any label. Sheila decided to take what she thought might be the uppers and leave the tranquillizers. She hoped that the unlabelled bottle did not carry heart pills or anything important and legal. But then if it did, Penelope would raise a fuss.

The first person Penelope saw when she entered the trailer which housed the restaurant was Gervase. She collected her food and went to join him.

'I am not happy with you,' she said, fixing the actor with a cold blue stare.

'*You're* not happy with *me*?' spluttered Gervase. 'You've ruined a morning's shoot with your silly behaviour. What's come over you, Penelope? You're like a spoilt brat.'

'I didn't ruin the morning's shoot. It was you, I gather, who got drunk and spilled the beans so that writer and that minister got to hear of it. I'm going to have a word with Harry. I can't act with you.'

'You're mad,' said Gervase, but suddenly frightened. He had been finding it harder and harder to get parts of late. 'I'll kill you. You'll be as dead as Jamie if you spoil my career.'

'I'm not frightened of you.' Penelope tossed her long blonde hair.

Gervase picked up his plate of food and, ignoring the startled looks from the others in the restaurant, sat down at a table as far away from her as possible.

It was unfortunate for Fiona that she was called to the phone to speak to the drama director of BBC Scotland just as Harry Frame arrived. Penelope hailed him as she left the restaurant. 'Come to my caravan, Harry,' she called.

He followed her in and sat down.

Penelope outlined what had happened that morning, ending up by saying she could not work with Gervase or Fiona or Sheila.

Harry fought down a rising feeling of panic. 'Look here,' he said. 'I can't go around firing everyone.'

'You were prepared to fire Fiona when Jamie asked you.'

Harry rose, his large bulk looming over her. 'And look what happened to him,' he said. 'I've taken enough. Get on with it, luv. Because it would be easier to replace you than either Fiona, Gervase or Sheila. There's plenty of little totties with good bodies and thin talent prepared to take your place.'

'Are you saying I can't act?'

He shrugged. 'You're no great shakes. Think about it.'

After he had gone, Penelope scrabbled in her handbag. Her pills had gone!

One of them must have taken them, but she couldn't very well complain. She swallowed a couple of tranquillizers. They couldn't really fire her. They wouldn't dare.


To everyone's relief, Penelope performed her part during the rest of the day without any awkward scenes. Her acting was a little wooden, but Giles decided to let it go for the sake of harmony.

By evening Penelope's tranquillizers had worn off, and she was feeling cross and irritable and hard done by.

Fiona was the one she hated the most. She wanted revenge. She had demanded that Fiona be fired, and that demand had been refused.

When she arrived in the dining room of the Tommel Castle Hotel that evening, she pointedly did not join the others but took a table on her own in a corner. She ordered trout and a bottle of champagne. After the others had left, she stayed in the dining room, finishing the bottle.

And then she heard a high, fluting English voice, saying, 'I am a trifle late, but I do not feel like cooking for myself tonight.'

Penelope looked up. Patricia Martyn-Broyd was being escorted to a table. Suddenly Penelope, elated and angry with champagne, thought she saw a way to get even with Fiona. She rose a trifle unsteadily to her feet and weaved between the tables in Patricia's direction, and came to a stop in front of her.

She leaned one hand on the table for support and said, 'You surely weren't taken in by that farce this morning, Patricia?'

'Well, at first it did look a little bit shocking, but after Fiona had explained it, I just had to accept that I am a bit behind the times.'

'You silly old cow,' said Penelope contemptuously, 'that scene with the nightwear was laid on for your benefit. The real scene, the screwing one, is the one that will be shown.'

'You must be lying!'

'Why should I bother? Instead of constantly complaining and interfering, you should be kissing our feet that your dreary books have got some recognition.'

'I shall get a lawyer tomorrow,' said Patricia, 'and get it stopped.'

Penelope shrugged. 'You can try. The reason you are shocked at the thought of naked bodies is because of the horrible one you've got yourself. I bet you have to hang a towel over the bathroom mirror.'

Patricia looked wildly around and saw the manager. 'Mr Johnson,' she called. 'Remove this person.'

'I'm going,' said Penelope, feeling all powerful. 'But I tell you this,' she said over her shoulder. 'You should save your money. You signed the contract and there's nothing you can do about it.'

After she had gone, Patricia sat at her table like a stone. The maître d' came up with the menu.

'What?' said Patricia in a dazed way.

'Are you ready to order, madam?'

'Yes ... no ... no, I am going home ... home.' Patricia stood up. She knocked her handbag to the floor, and the contents scattered over the carpet. She knelt and began to pick them up. Jenkins, the maître d', stooped to help her.

He remembered afterwards, when questioned by the police, that Miss Martyn-Broyd had been weeping.

To Fiona's relief, it was a very subdued Penelope who reported for work at seven the following morning. The scene of the chase across the mountain was to be reshot. The sun had gone and the day was misty, all colours bleached out of the landscape.

'Won't the mist be too thick up on the mountain?' Fiona asked the director.

'It's supposed to lift later,' said Giles, 'and we might get some good atmospheric shots.'

Once the helicopters had everyone up on the heathery plateau, they all climbed out. Sheila felt there was something wrong in being in the same place where Jamie had been murdered. Mist swirled around. Sometimes it lifted and she could see everyone clearly, and then it closed down again.

'We'll just do the running shot,' said the director when everything was set up. 'Perhaps it won't work with this mist. You start from here, Penelope, and run over to the edge and stop short.'

'Isn't that where Jamie was murdered?' asked Penelope.

'No, he was murdered over there. Sheila, go over to that crag and show her where to stand.'

Sheila obediently trotted off. The mist lifted again like a curtain being raised, and they could see Sheila standing on an outcrop of rock.

'You'll come to a stop right here, Penelope,' Sheila called back. 'Then you stand and shield your eyes and look down the mountain.'

'Wait there a minute,' Giles called.

Sheila stood where she was. A shaft of sunlight suddenly lit up the village of Drim, standing beside the black loch. The air was pure and clean and scented with wild thyme.

'All right,' she heard Giles shout. 'You can come back now.'

Sheila walked back. 'So, Penelope, in your own time,' said Giles, 'start running and then stop just where Sheila was.'

'Mist's closing down again,' said Fiona.

'I know,' said Giles. 'But I just want to try one shot and see what she looks like disappearing into the mist.'

Penelope was wearing a long scarlet dress which floated about her excellent body.

They all took up their positions. 'Right,' said Giles softly, 'when you're ready, Penelope. Quiet, everyone. And . . . action!'

Penelope ran off into the mist as fleet as a deer. She disappeared into the thickening mist. There was a silence.

Then suddenly there was a high, wailing, descending scream.

'She's fallen!' screamed Sheila.

'Not her,' said Giles dryly. 'Just playing silly games. Go and get her, Sheila. Fiona! . . . Where's Fiona?'

Sheila ran forward. She reached the outcrop. There was no sign of Penelope.

'Penelope!' she shouted.

At first there was no sound at all, and then she heard a faint moan coming from far below her.

Then the mist lifted again and she saw Penelope spread out on a rock a dizzying distance below the outcrop.

'Oh, God, she has fallen!' she screamed. 'Get help! Phone Hamish Macbeth!'

As if in mockery, the mist lifted entirely and the sun blazed down.


Harry Frame, Fiona, Giles and the production manager, Hal Forsyth, sat huddled in Fiona's office in Drim Castle.

'Her family are going to sue the life out of us,' muttered Harry Frame.

The phone rang, making them all jump. Fiona picked it up and listened. Then she said in a bleak voice after she had replaced the receiver. 'That was Sheila from the hospital in Inverness. Penelope's dead. She died on arrival.'

'Shit!' said Harry Frame bitterly. 'Time's running out. We'll need to get a new actress, coach her. Winter comes here early.'

Major Neal put his head round the door. 'Police,' he announced.

Startled faces turned in the direction of the door.

Detective Chief Inspector Blair lumbered in, followed by Macnab and Anderson.

'Penelope Gates is dead,' he said.

'We know,' said Fiona. 'We've just heard the news from the hospital.'

'PC Hamish Macbeth went down to the hospital in the helicopter with her. She said something to him afore she died. She said, "Someone caught my ankle and pulled me over." So we're looking at a case of murder!'

'We'd better talk about this,' said Hamish as he left Raigmore Hospital in Inverness with Sheila. 'Let's have a quick meal before we go back.'

They took a taxi to a small restaurant in the centre of Inverness which was self-service. When they had collected their food and found a table, Hamish asked, 'Who wanted her dead?'

'Everyone,' said Sheila. Her eyes filled with tears. 'It was such a dreadful day yesterday.' She slowly began to tell him everything that had happened. 'Fiona said she had a good mind to tell you about her suspicions that Penelope was on uppers so you could arrest her.'

'I probably wouldn't have, not having arrested Fiona herself for smoking pot,' said Hamish. 'I sometimes wonder why they have laws banning soft drugs when we're supposed to turn a blind eye to them. Look at New York. They started this zero tolerance business, clearing up all the lesser crimes like mugging and graffiti, and it's been a big success. They feel if they begin at the bottom and start clearing up the soft drugs, the harder ones might become less common. A businessman can be in bad trouble if he's been drinking and he's only a little over the limit, but anyone can smoke themselves silly with pot. But, my God, mention arresting anyone for smoking pot, and you'll have every liberal in the country down on your neck. Arrest a man for having drunk a little bit over the limit, and it's "Well done, Officer."

'So she threatened, or so you heard, to get rid of you, Fiona and Gervase. What had Harry Frame to say about that?'

'We don't know,' said Sheila. 'He just said he didn't want to talk about it.'

'So as far as Fiona and the rest of you were concerned, he may have been thinking of sacking you?'

'Yes . . . well, no. He couldn't have got rid of three people.' Her eyes again filled with tears. 'I think I'll hear that scream of Penelope's as she went over until the day I die.'

'And Patricia? She believed that silly explanation about the nude scene?'

'Oh, yes, she was all soothed down and happy when she left.'

'The trouble is,' said Hamish, 'in the Highlands everything gets out sooner or later. You say something to someone in private, and before you know it, the whole village has heard about it the next day.'

Sheila wiped her eyes with the back of her hand and tried to smile. 'In that case, murders should be easy to solve.'

146

'That's a different thing. When there's a murder, everyone feels guilty and clams up. It's odd, but all the innocent people start getting shifty about where they were and what they were doing.'

Sheila turned a trifle pale. 'I must be the number one suspect. I could have pushed her over and then pretended she fell.'

'But Penelope herself said someone caught hold of her ankle and pulled her over. Someone must have been lurking around in the mist, waiting for an opportunity. Where was Fiona?'

'She was with Giles Brown, the director, and then she disappeared in the mist for a bit.'

'At least Gervase wasn't about.'

'But he was,' said Sheila.

'Why?'

'Because the chief inspector is the murderer.'

'How do they work that out?'

'He's obsessed with Lady Harriet and murders her butler so that he can get her up from England to investigate.'

'But he gets into bed with her.'

'Well, she's supposed to seduce him to find out what he knows.'

'And where does the rising tide come in?'

'The butler's body is found on the beach, and Lady Harriet judges the time of death from the high tide mark.'

'I believe Patricia's book got quite good reviews.'

'When you read it, it's all convoluted and sounds convincing, although her style is a bit wordy and precious for me. What does "pathic" mean?'

'Don't know. Give me a sentence.'

'"She gave him a pathic smile." I looked it up. It said victim, catamite, passive. Could mean she smiled like a victim or gave a passive smile. Can't be a catamite smile, surely? I agree with Orwell: if you have to look up words in the dictionary, don't use them.'

'Maybe Patricia didn't have to look it up in the dictionary.'

'Maybe. What happens now?'

'I drive you back to Drim, where the police will interrogate you. The press tonight will be followed tomorrow by the world's press: "Beautiful Actress Murdered". Blair will be under intense pressure. Remember that and just answer calmly.'

'How do we get back? They'll hardly fly us there in a helicopter.'

Hamish took out a mobile telephone. 'Inverness police'll get us back.'


They were driven straight back to Drim Castle. Major Neal had the fire lit in the main hall because, although the weather was warm outside and still light because it was at the time of the year when it hardly ever got dark, the castle was cold and gloomy.

Jimmy Anderson came out to meet Hamish and Sheila. 'Follow me,' he said to Sheila. 'Mr Blair wants a word with ye.'

Hamish would have liked to accompany her but was sure that Blair would order him away. He joined the party round the fire. Most of the television crew seemed to be there.

Harry Frame scowled at Hamish. Then he said, 'I say we go on. We can't let all this publicity go for nothing. We'll raise money selling that last shot of Penelope to every television company from here to Moscow.'

'Aren't the police hanging on to that?' asked Hamish.

'Got several copies,' said Harry. He turned to Fiona. 'What about Mary Hoyle?'

'She's a fine actress, but no tottie, nor will she shed her clothes.'

'I'm fed up with totties. I want a good, solid actress to pull us through this. You know her reputation. She's got a photographic memory. Also, she's not doing anything at the moment.'

'I'd settle for anyone who would keep their mouth shut and just work. But can we really go on?'

'Of course we go on,' said Harry. 'With all this publicity, by the time it goes out, we'll have a huge audience.'

The door of the castle opened and a woman police officer led Patricia in. She looked white and tired and had lost all her usual confidence.

'Wait here until they're ready for you,' ordered the policewoman.

Patricia sat down at the edge of the group, clutching her large handbag.

A silence fell. Patricia was a writer and not one of them. Hamish took his chair round and sat next to her.

'You'll be asked where you were today,' he said.

'It's difficult to prove,' said Patricia miserably. She started and dropped her handbag as Jenkins, the maître d' from the hotel, came in. 'What's he doing here?' she hissed.

Hamish rose and went forward.

'I don't want you,' said Jenkins, arms as usual slightly akimbo, as if carrying an imaginary tray. 'I want the man in charge. It's important.'

Glad of an excuse to get into that interviewing room and rescue Sheila, Hamish nodded and left the hall. The interviewing was taking place in Fiona's office. Blair stopped in mid-bark and glared at Hamish. 'Whit dae ye want?'

'Jenkins, the maître d' from the Tommel Castle Hotel, is here. He says he has information for you.'

Blair's eyes gleamed. 'Send him in. I'll talk more to you later, Miss Burford. Don't leave.'

Hamish went out with Sheila. 'Bad time?' he asked sympathetically.

'It was awful. He practically accused me of the murder.'

'That's his way. He's aye trying to fright a confession out of someone or other, and I've neffer known it to work.'

Sheila joined the others at the fire, and Hamish signalled to Jenkins. He was determined to stay in the interviewing room and hear what the man had to say.

So when Jenkins took a seat in front of the desk facing Blair, Hamish slid to a corner of the room and sat down.

Jenkins introduced himself.

'So what have ye to tell us?' demanded Blair.

'I was on duty in the castle dining room last night,' said Jenkins. 'Miss Penelope Gates had dinner on her own. She ordered a bottle of champagne and drank the lot. Then she saw that writer, Miss Martyn-Broyd, come in. I gather from gossip that there was apparently some sex scene and Miss Martyn-Broyd and Mr Jessop, the minister, had been reassured it was not so. Miss Gates told Miss Martyn-Broyd that she had been tricked, that there was in fact a sex scene, and she called her books dreary. Miss Martyn-Broyd was distressed and weeping. To my way of thinking,' said Jenkins pompously, 'her mind was so overset that she probably murdered Miss Gates.'

'If that's all ye've got to say,' said Blair, looking at him with dislike, 'ye can go.'

Jenkins departed in a huff.

'Has that writer woman arrived yet?' demanded Blair.

'Yes,' said Hamish.

Blair glared at him for a moment, as if debating whether to tell him that he should not be in the interviewing room, but then said, 'Fetch her in.'

Jimmy Anderson went out. Hamish stayed where he was.

Patricia came in. She was quite white, but now composed.

Blair started the questioning in his usual unsubtle way.

'Where were you today?'

'At what time, Officer?'

'Chief Inspector. We'll start with when you got up.'

'I made breakfast and wrote another few pages of my new book. Then I went out for a drive.'

'Where?'

'I was distressed over what the television people were doing with my book. I know Miss Gates is dead and *de mortuis* and all that, but she was a horrible, vicious and vulgar woman. She sneered at me in the Tommel Castle Hotel the evening before and told me that what I had been assured was not going to be a pornographic scene was in fact going to be just that. She said they had tricked me into believing it otherwise. I was very, very upset. I could not write properly. So I drove and drove mind-

lessly. I had planned to drive to Drim and confront them, but I had no courage left. I do not
know where I drove or for how long, but I
suddenly realized I was hungry. I found
myself in Golspie and went to the Sutherland
Arms Hotel for a bar lunch. Then I returned
home.'

'We'll check with the Sutherland Arms
Hotel. What is the make and registration number of your car?'

Patricia gave it to him.

'The way I see it,' said Blair with a fat smile,
'is that you, more than anyone else, had a good
reason to want Penelope Gates dead. She had
jeered at you about how you had been tricked,
and you admit your mind was overset. So
you went to Drim and you climbed up that
mountain. You heard Penelope being instructed to stand on that rock. You scrambled
around in the mist until you were underneath
and then you grabbed her ankle and pulled
her over.'

'That is ridiculous,' said Patricia coolly. 'May
I point out that it is now after midnight and I
am very tired.'

Blair struck the desk. 'We're all bloody tired,
woman! But you will stay here until ah'm
finished with you.' His Glasgow accent, which
he usually modified when speaking to the
'toffs' such as Jenkins and Patricia, suddenly
thickened.

\* \* \*

Sheila sat in the hall with the others and waited. She was feeling hard done by. It had transpired that the company lawyers had been present when all the others had been interviewed, but to her complaint Harry had given a massive shrug and said the lawyers needed their sleep.

For the first time, Sheila began to wonder who had really murdered Penelope. It was no longer an intellectual exercise. One of them in this castle, probably one of them around the fire, had murdered Penelope. No one was mourning her; no one had a good word to say for her.


Hamish Macbeth awoke the next morning as the alarm shrilled. He felt very tired. He had had about four hours' sleep.

He ran over in his mind the events of the night before. Fiona said she had been nowhere near Penelope, but there was no proof of that. Gervase had no firm alibi. With the mist so thick, anyone could have been anywhere.

He wondered if the BBC would go for a new actress and changed script or if the whole thing would just fall through.

He rose and washed and dressed. He then went into the kitchen to prepare himself some breakfast. Rain drummed steadily down outside, the first rain for many days.

There was a tentative knock at the door. He sighed. Probably some local looking for gossip. But when he opened the door, it was to find Patricia Martyn-Broyd.

'I must speak to you, Hamish,' she said. There were black circles under her eyes, panda-like against the parchment of her old skin.

'Come in,' he said. 'I was just preparing breakfast. Can I be getting you something?'

'I couldn't eat a thing,' said Patricia.

'Sit yourself down anyway and have a coffee.'

Patricia waited while Hamish prepared two cups of coffee and then sat down at the kitchen table opposite her.

'I am in bad trouble,' said Patricia.

'Why? What's happened?'

She looked at him impatiently. 'I am suspected of murdering that creature.'

'That's Blair's way. He goes on as if he suspects everyone.'

'But don't you see! I am the one with the strongest motive.'

'I don't know about that. She had threatened to get Fiona King, Gervase Hart and Sheila Burford fired. And they were all up on the mountain with her. Also, Harry Frame let slip last night that there had been some change of mind at BBC Scotland and they wanted more of a traditional detective series, in which case Penelope and her beautiful body would not have been needed all that much. But then,

I hardly think Harry Frame would shove her over a cliff to get rid of her. If you have not murdered Penelope Gates, then you have nothing to worry about.'

'I am not stupid!' said Patricia. 'I came here to get your help and to get away from the press. I have no alibi, and that man Blair, under pressure from the media, is determined to make an arrest, any arrest. I want you, Hamish Macbeth, to find out who really murdered Penelope.'

'Why me?'

'I formed the opinion that you are not lacking in intelligence. From the church gossip at Cnothan, I discovered that you had solved crimes before, and all on your own initiative.'

'I will do my best, of course, to find out who did it,' said Hamish cautiously. 'But I do not have the resources of Strathbane.'

'Nonetheless, I am relying on you. I am not a poor woman. I can pay you.'

'That's not necessary. May I suggest if you don't want any breakfast that you go home and get some sleep?'

'I can't with all those press around.'

'As you have pointed out, you're not a poor woman. Take a room at the hotel. They'll have the keepers posted at the gates to keep the press out.'

'I shall do that. Will you keep me informed of any developments?'

'I'll tell you what I can, but I would suggest you try to remember where you were driving. Someone might have seen you.'

When she left, he fried himself some bacon and eggs. He did not have any newspaper delivered, usually buying one at Patel's. The tabloids would be having a field day publishing naked pictures of Penelope. It was as well that husband of hers was dead.

The phone rang constantly in the police office, and each time the answering machine clicked on. Calls from the press.

Then a truculent call from Blair. 'I know you're there, you lazy Hielan hound. Pick up that writer woman and bring her back here. Move your arse.'

Hamish sighed. Poor Patricia. And yet why should he think poor Patricia? The woman was armoured in rigid pride. But she was also lonely and vulnerable under that carapace. He finished his breakfast, checked on his sheep and hens and set out to collect Patricia.

# Chapter Six

*Nay, Nay! You must not hastily
To such conclusions jump.*
— Lewis Carroll

'Don't you want to get a lawyer?' asked Hamish Macbeth as he drove Patricia towards Drim.

'I hate lawyers,' said Patricia, stifling a yawn. 'Oh, why did that wretched man want to see me now? I could have done with a few hours' sleep.'

'Once your interrogation is over,' said Hamish, 'it might be a good idea if you just get on with your writing and forget about the television thing. All this has been driving you frantic.'

'But not enough to murder anyone,' said Patricia sharply. 'People of my generation do not murder.'

Hamish thought briefly of several well-known murderers of Patricia's generation but refrained from telling her about them. He was glad of an opportunity to go to Drim again to see what he could find out.

But he found he was not being allowed to sit in on the interview with Patricia. 'We've got enough people here,' snarled Blair.

Hamish wandered outside the castle. Sheila came up to him. Her bright blue eyes looked up into his own. 'There's something you should know,' she said in a low voice. 'Let's go somewhere private.'

They walked past various members of the television company, most of whom seemed to have mobile phones glued to their ears. 'Do they need to use these phones so much?' asked Hamish curiously. 'Mobile phone calls are expensive.'

'You know what we say in the business?' said Sheila wryly. 'If we don't use our mobile phones at least every fifteen minutes, our self-esteem drops.'

They walked towards the village. Various members of the press were circling around like jackals, cameramen lugged their equipment, television news crews had their vans parked along the road leading to the castle.

'What a circus,' said Sheila. 'How long will they stay?'

'A few days,' said Hamish, 'and then some other news will take them all away.' He looked around. 'No one about. So what do you have to tell me?'

'Well, don't let anyone know where you got

this information from. Harry Frame called us all together and said none of us were to talk to the police or the press. We should all stick together.'

'So what's your news?'

'Some of the crew were in the restaurant and heard Penelope telling Gervase she wouldn't act with him any longer.'

'We know that.'

'But Gervase was heard threatening to kill her.'

They walked on in silence. Then Hamish said, 'It might mean nothing at all. People get angry and say, "I'll kill you," quite a lot. She said she would get you fired. Did you threaten to kill her?'

'No, of course not . . . Oh, my God!'

'You did?'

'I had a row with her, and as I left her caravan, I shouted, "I hope you break your neck." I was thinking about the shoot up on the mountain, which was scheduled for the following day.'

'I can't help thinking about the first murder,' said Hamish slowly. 'I'm uneasy about that.'

'You think Josh didn't do it?'

'The only evidence is that blood on his hands. Blair was so keen to wrap the thing up that he didn't look any further.'

'But I heard that Josh was shouting, "I'll kill him," by two policemen in St Vincent Street in Glasgow.'

'That's puzzling me. He sees a photo of his wife, naked, on the book jacket advertisement, and yet he says, "I'll kill him."'

'Jamie's name was on the back of the book jacket as scriptwriter, I gather.'

'But why should Josh immediately decide that Jamie was to blame? What about Harry Frame?'

'We'll never know.'

'Wait a bit. Can I use your mobile?' asked Hamish.

'I thought you had one.'

'But I can't really charge for this call.'

She fished her phone out of her handbag and handed it to him. 'Be my guest.'

Hamish sat down on a rock at the side of the road, and Sheila sank down into the heather beside the rock.

Hamish phoned directory enquiries and got the telephone number of John Smith's bookshop. Then he phoned the bookshop, identified himself and asked to speak to the assistant who had served Josh.

'Liz Turnbull,' said a voice after a wait.

'Miss Turnbull,' said Hamish, 'I am Police Constable Hamish Macbeth of Lochdubh in Sutherland. You served Josh Gates with an ordnance survey map?'

'The man who killed that scriptwriter. Yes. He was in a right taking.'

'Now outside on the street, two policemen heard him subsequently say, "I'll kill him."'

There was a silence, and then Liz Turnbull said, 'Her. He said "her".'

'How do you know?'

'One of the assistants was coming back from his break. He told me.'

'Could I speak to him?'

'Sure, hold on.'

Hamish waited. From the other end of the phone came the noisy sounds of a busy bookshop. Then a man's voice said, 'Yes?'

'This is PC Hamish Macbeth. And you are . . .?'

'Hugh Roy.'

'Mr Roy, I gather that you overheard Josh Gates out in the street saying, "I'll kill her."'

'Yes, I was just coming back from my break.'

'But I wass told he said "him". "I'll kill him."'

'No, it was definitely "her". He was shouting.'

Hamish phoned Strathbane police headquarters and asked if he could speak to one of the policemen who had been in St Vincent Street that day. He was in luck. One of the policemen was in the canteen, and Hamish waited patiently while he was brought to the phone.

'Aye, I 'member it well,' said the policeman. 'It's in the report I filed.'

'Did Josh Gates say, "I'll kill her", or "I'll kill him"?'

'"I'll kill her."'

Hamish thanked him. He turned to Sheila.

'Josh shouted, "I'll kill her." Why should Jimmy Anderson say otherwise?'

'Maybe Glasgow police made a mistake on the report.'

'I doubt it. It iss beginning to look to me as if Blair were too anxious to wrap it all up. If anyone iss looking for me, tell them I've been called back to Lochdubh.'

Hamish loped off at a fast trot, leaving Sheila to make her way more slowly back to the castle.

Once in the police station at Lochdubh, he sat down in front of his computer and stared at it. On a previous case, someone had broken into Blair's records at Strathbane by guessing his password. Blair would have changed the password since then. Hamish ran through every swear word he could think of, without success. How could he get the right password?

He phoned Drim Castle and asked to speak to Detective Jimmy Anderson. He was told the detective was in the interviewing room but he said he had new and important information.

Jimmy at last came to the phone. 'This had better be good, Hamish.'

'I'm getting a bottle of the best malt whisky in for you.'

'I'll be there to drink it as soon as I can. So what do I have to do for it?'

'Give me Blair's password.'

'Come on, man. How would I know it, anyway?'

'Because he's a blabbermouth when he's drunk. Come on, Jimmy.'

'Why do you want it?'

'I'm on to something. Think of this. I haff solved the cases afore and let that fat slob take the credit. What if I wass to solve this one and let you have all the glory?'

There was a long silence. Then Jimmy whispered, 'Okay. It's balls.'

'That wass the one oath I didnae try. Thanks, Jimmy.'

'I'll be down later to see what you're on to.'

Hamish sat down at the computer again. Once into Blair's reports, he flipped them rapidly down the screen until he came to the Glasgow policemen's report. He leaned back. It was quite clear. Josh had definitely said, 'I'll kill her.' He leaned forward and ran the report on. Then he stopped and stared at the screen. On his way north, Josh had stopped at a bed-and-breakfast called Costa Brava outside Perth. At breakfast he had been heard to shout, 'He'll have me to reckon with!'

Hamish sat back again. So Josh had last been heard threatening a *man*.

He was disappointed. He was wasting time. What if Josh had been first heard threatening a woman? Penelope was murdered after he himself had died. Time to get back to the present murder.

Blair had not sent through all the reports yet. Hamish would just need to wait and hope that, unlike last time, Blair would not know that his reports had been broken into.

He went into his living room and crouched in front of the bookshelves. The bottom shelf contained a series of ordnance survey maps. He opened the one covering the Drim area and spread it out on the floor. Was there any other way up that mountain? Was there any way other than the path he had used himself?

He frowned. Angus Macdonald, the seer, was once a famous climber.

Angus claimed to be able to foretell the future. Hamish did not believe in his powers, judging that any successful predictions were the result of shrewdness and listening to gossip. But there was the very superstitious Highland side of Hamish which made him uneasy around the old man.

Angus expected everyone who visited to bring him some sort of present. Hamish scowled. He already had to buy a bottle of good malt for Jimmy. He went into Patel's. There was a display of Dundee cake, 'great reduction'. Hamish bought one and set out for the seer's cottage.

'There's aye a cheap streak in you, Hamish Macbeth,' said Angus sourly as he accepted the cake. Hamish realized the seer probably knew it had been on sale at a reduced price.

He followed Angus into his old-fashioned cottage, where a peat fire smouldered in the hearth.

Angus, looking more like one of the minor prophets than ever with his grey beard and thick, long grey hair, said, 'I suppose ye've come to find out who murdered the lassie.'

'And I suppose you know?'

'Oh, aye, I ken fine.' Angus half-closed his eyes. 'I see a wumman wi' short hair and big boots.'

'A young woman?' asked Hamish, thinking of Sheila. 'Blonde hair?'

'No, she is about forty, dark hair, takes drugs.'

Fiona, thought Hamish.

'How d'you know she takes drugs?'

'I see it here,' said Angus, tapping his forehead and reminding Hamish of a Tenniel illustration of the eagle in *Alice's Adventures in Wonderland*.

Hamish was wise to the ways of the seer. When he had been sniffing for pot, one of the Drim gamekeepers had been hanging around the castle hall. Everyone told Angus everything.

'And why should she kill the lassie?' asked Hamish, humouring him.

'Because she iss ambitious and thon Penelope was out to ruin her career.'

'Come on, Angus,' said Hamish. 'Why are you so definite? I mean, it's not like you to name names. You usually hint . . . "I see a dark woman", that kind of thing.'

'Och, no, Hamish, you haff always doubted the power.'

'Forget about your powers for the moment, Angus. What I really came about was to find if you knew of another path up that mountain, maybe from the back. You know we usually use that path which runs up between thon two cliffs.'

Angus looked huffy. 'I think you will need to be doing better than a piece of old Dundee cake if you want mair information.'

'Now, look here, Angus,' said Hamish sharply. 'I could have you up for obstructing the police in their enquiries.'

The seer sat in stubborn silence. Hamish sighed.

'Look, Angus, I've got some fine trout in the freezer, six of them. You can have them if you come off it and tell me about any path up that mountain.'

Angus rose to his feet and ferreted in a box in the corner. He came back with some sheets of paper and then placed them on the table and took out a pen.

'Come here, Hamish,' he said. He started to make a rough sketch. 'There's a wee path here. Not many people know about it. It starts here on the lower slopes and twists and turns like a rabbit track, but it gives you even easier access than the other one.'

Hamish watched the quickly moving pen. 'If it's that easy, why don't more people use it?'

Angus said, 'You know how it is. Climbers like a difficult climb, and the locals neffer go up there. Why should they? I mean, local people don't go mountain climbing. It's only the oddball like me and the tourists. And talking of the tourists, they get sillier every year. Down in Glencoe in the winter, you haff to keep ducking, for they are falling off the mountain like dead flies. No respect for the Scottish weather. Up they go, down comes the blizzard, out comes the mountain rescue and the taxpayer foots the bill. Then some silly bugger who's cost the nation a fortune sells his story of "How I Survived" to the tabloids and keeps the money. If I had my way –'

'All right, all right,' said Hamish, cutting short the lecture. 'I'll take this map and I'll let you have thae trout by tonight.'

He made his way to the door.

'Hamish!' called Angus.

Hamish turned round. 'Aye?'

'It iss no use you getting your hopes up about that pretty little blonde lassie. Ambition will get her chust the way it got the Fiona woman. Be careful there, Hamish.'

'Oh, aye,' said Hamish cynically. 'I'll be leaving you to look at your crystal balls.'

As he strode off, he wondered if the police had found that other path.


Eileen Jessop sat at her dressing table in the manse in Drim and looked dismally at her reflection in the mirror. She felt she had not really looked at herself properly in years. Her eyes blinked back at her through her thick glasses. She studied her iron grey hair and her dumpy figure.

She had been a pretty girl when she had got married all those years ago ... well, she had thought she was pretty. But somehow, right after they were married, Colin Jessop had begun to frown on anything he thought of as frivolous in the way of clothes and hairstyles. Make-up was definitely out, not at all the thing for a minister's wife.

At first she had stood up to him, but he had gradually become more bullying, more aggressive, until slowly her personality had become submerged under his. It was so much easier to give in, to bend to his will, than face another of those angry scenes she had come to dread.

When he had been preaching at a church in Edinburgh, life had been easier. She had friends in the parish, she could go to theatres and cinemas. But he had resented her having any sort of independent life. When he had accepted the position of minister in Drim, Eileen had felt her very last little bit of freedom had been taken from her.

She had felt isolated and shy. There was an odd sort of pecking order in a Highland village, and the minister's wife was expected to keep a kind of distance between herself and the ordinary village woman. Until the idea of the film, she had not known any of the women very well. Normally Colin Jessop might have objected, but he had recently been spending a great deal of time during the week in either Strathbane or Inverness on what he described as 'religious business'.

For the first time in years, Eileen was free of his demanding and bullying company for long periods and felt that something inside her spirit was beginning to grow, giving her a restless spring-like feeling.

And yet, she thought, looking at herself, her appearance only reflected the old Eileen. It would be grand to go down to Alice and get her awful, awful dull grey hair dyed. But then he would notice and there would be a scene; he might even stop her film, and she could not bear that. She had a great deal of tape. Eileen wanted to ask someone in the television company for advice about cutting and editing. Colin had forbidden her to go near them, and so far she had obeyed him. But she could approach one of them when he was away.

There was a ring at the doorbell and she went to answer it. It was Ailsa Kennedy. She and Eileen had quickly formed an odd sort of friendship.

'Come in,' said Eileen. 'What brings you? I thought you would be watching all the detectives and police.'

'It's half day at the shop,' said Ailsa. 'I was thinking of taking the car for a drive into

Inverness. Jock doesn't need it today. Fancy coming along?'

Eileen brightened, and then her face fell. 'Colin likes me to be here when he gets back, and I never know when that's going to be. And he always likes dinner to be ready for him. But I've actually cooked a stew for tonight. It would only need to be heated up.'

'Then leave him a note to tell him to heat it,' said Ailsa.

'Oh, I c-couldn't do that.'

'Why not?' demanded Ailsa, tossing her red hair.

'He'd be so very angry.'

'Husbands are always angry. That's their nature, and the nature of us women is not to pay a blind bit o' notice.'

A little spark of rebellion ignited somewhere in Eileen's brain. Ailsa was always talking about 'us women', making the lonely minister's wife feel she now belonged to a freemasonry of women who were not afraid of their husbands.

'I'll go,' she said. 'Wait till I leave a note.'

Ailsa glanced in amusement at the minister's wife as she drove competently along the single-track roads, for Eileen was singing 'These Boots Are Made for Walking'.

Then Eileen broke off singing and asked suddenly, 'What do you think of my hair?'

'Very nice,' said Ailsa with true Highland politeness.

'I hate it, hate it,' said Eileen passionately. 'I hate being dumpy, and I hate having grey hair.'

'Then that is easily solved,' said Ailsa. 'We'll drop in at a hairdresser's in Inverness and you can get it done. You don't want to go to Alice. I don't know what dyes she uses, but she still turns out bottle blondes or dead, lifeless black. Your figure's probably not that bad. You just need new clothes. Does he keep you on a tight budget?'

'No, I've a bit of money of my own.'

'There you are, then.'

'He'll be so angry.'

'Of course he will. They always are. It's their way,' said Ailsa sententiously, as if explaining the strange ways of some native tribe up the Amazon. 'Take it from me, you do what you want, they rave, and after a few days, they forget what you looked like afore. Now, seeing as how you're getting your hair done, we may as well have the top down.'

Ailsa was driving an old Morris Minor with a soft top. She pulled to the side of the road and folded back the roof.

Then they sped off in the sunlight again.

Eileen was to remember that journey for the rest of her life, the wind tearing through her hair and sending hairpins flying back on the road. Ailsa had put noisy pop music in the tape deck, and they sailed over the bridge from the Black Isle into Inverness, all racing wind and vulgar music and Eileen feeling young for the first time in her life.

Ailsa parked in the multi-storey car park at the bus station. 'Hairdresser first,' said Ailsa, 'and then we'll have a late lunch.'

The hairdresser Ailsa led Eileen to was a new one, quite terrifying to one timid minister's wife. But the girls were Highland and so had that gentle friendliness and entered into the interesting business of choosing colour and a hairstyle for Eileen.

Two hours later, Eileen emerged blinking into the sunlight. Her hair was black and shining and cut in a smooth style. She clung to Ailsa's arm and kept glancing at her new appearance in shop windows. Ailsa came to a sudden stop. 'Thon's a grand dress for you.'

Eileen looked at it. It was a conventional shirtwaister but of soft silk, with a swirling pattern of peacock greens, golds and blue. She took a deep breath. 'I'll buy it.'

Ailsa insisted she wear it, and then they walked to a restaurant which Ailsa said was open all afternoon because all the normal lunchtime places had closed.

The restaurant was all brass and mahogany and palm trees and an exotic menu of foreign dishes. They ordered a Mexican dish and washed it down with lager, Ailsa protesting that she would 'walk off the drink' after lunch.

Most of the tables were screened from the others by greenery and brass poles. Eileen said she had to go to the ladies' room. She actually wanted to study her new appearance in the mirror.

It was as she was walking to the ladies' room that she suddenly saw her husband. He was sitting at a table by the window. Opposite him was a plump middle-aged woman with improbably blonde hair and a predatory rouged mouth. Colin was holding this woman's hand across the table and, noticed Eileen in amazement, he had a soppy smile on his face.

She scurried on into the ladies' room and leaned against the hand basin. Colin, of all people! This probably explained all his trips to Inverness. What should she do? Nothing. Ailsa would know.

Her black hair and new dress gave her a strange courage. She took out a lipstick that she had bought in Boots and applied it carefully. She had also bought eye shadow, mascara, foundation cream and powder but decided she was too shaken to put on anything else.

A few weeks before, a time in her life which Eileen privately designated as Before the Film, she would have kept secret the news of her husband's presence in the restaurant and possible infidelity.

But she was enjoying this new friendship, this new feeling of not being alone, so as soon as she was back at the table, she blurted out, 'Ailsa! Ailsa, you'll never believe what has happened, what I've just seen. Colin! My husband! He's in this very restaurant, and he's holding hands with a trollopy woman.'

'Whit!' Ailsa shrieked.

'Keep your voice down,' whispered Eileen urgently. 'Colin is over there near the bar, holding hands with a blonde woman.'

'It could be some parishioner that he is consoling.'

'You didn't see the look on his face.'

'Crivens!' said Ailsa. 'That wee man. I'd never have believed it. Did he see your hair?'

Eileen shook her head. 'He was too wrapped up in that woman.'

'Are you going over there to confront him?'

There was a silence while Eileen looked down at her hands. Then she said, 'No, I'm not.'

'But you'll speak to him this evening?'

'Maybe not.'

Ailsa looked at her curiously. 'You look a bit shocked, but not furious or distressed.'

Eileen gave a small smile. 'Maybe I'm in shock.'

Ailsa took a meditative sip of a blue cocktail called Highland Wind, tilting her head so that the little tartan umbrella sticking out of the top of the concoction did not get in her eye.

'It's a rare piece of gossip.'

'You're not to talk about it,' said Eileen fiercely, 'not to Jock, not to anyone.'

'All right.'

'Promise?'

'Cross my heart.'

'We'd best take our time until Colin leaves,' said Eileen. 'Do you know what amazes me?'

'What? I thought the whole business of Colin being maybe unfaithful to you would be enough puzzlement.'

'That woman is wearing a ton of make-up and dyed hair, yet if I put on so much as lipstick, he shouts at me that it is not fitting for the wife of a minister.'

'Oh, that doesn't puzzle me at all,' said Ailsa. 'Men were aye the same. The minute they've got you, they start to try to get rid of all the things about you that attracted them to you in the first place.'

And despite her bewilderment at her husband's behaviour, Eileen felt once more enfolded in the world of women, a world banded together against the peculiar alien world of men.

It took Hamish Macbeth some time to find Angus's path. At last he located it and found his way up the mountain, searching all the while for clues. But by the time he had nearly reached the top, an easier climb than the other path, he found to his surprise, he had found nothing at all. The path looked as if no one had used it for years but rabbits and deer.

Still, anyone using the path could have easily reached the bit under that outcrop of rock. But how would anyone know Penelope was to stand there? Was it in the script?

He thought after some reflection that the murder had not been premeditated. Either Fiona or Gervase or Harry had seen the opportunity to get rid of her and had taken it. Right under the outcrop was a flat, sheltered bit where someone could have stood. Harry could have easily slid down there, reached up and pulled Penelope's ankle to overbalance her. Fiona could have run off in the mist and done the same, or Gervase. And where had Patricia really been that day, and was her plea to him for help merely a blind?

Could the seer really think that Fiona had done it? If so, who had supplied him with that information? Angus rarely went out these days, but picked up gossip from his visitors. From time to time there were articles in the newspapers on 'the seer of the Highlands', and he had been on television several times.

He noticed how clearly he could hear all the voices of the men still searching the heathery plateau above.

Anyone lurking down here could have heard the instructions to Penelope.

He made his way back down the mountain and headed for Drim Castle to learn that Patricia had been taken off to Strathbane for further questioning. The information was supplied by Fiona.

'So what happens now?' asked Hamish.

'To Patricia?'

'No, to the TV show.'

'We go on. Mary Hoyle is flying up today. She's a competent actress.'

'I've seen her in some things. Hardly a blonde bombshell.'

'It'll take a few alterations to the script, but we'll manage.'

Hamish studied her for a few moments and then asked, 'Do you think Patricia did it?'

'Yes, I do,' said Fiona, puffing on a cigarette which Hamish was pleased to note was ordinary tobacco.

'Why?'

Fiona put down her cigarette and ran her hands through her short-cropped hair. 'None of us could have done it. I've worked with all these people before. It's not in them. But writers! Take it from me, they're all mad with vanity. They don't understand how television works, and they expect us to dramatize every dreary word they've written.'

'It could be argued that murder is not in Patricia, either. She is very conscious of being a lady.'

'"God bless the squire and his relations, and keep them in their proper stations",' quoted Fiona.

'Aye, something like that. Is Sheila around?'

'She's been taken to Strathbane for questioning as well. She was heard shouting to Penelope, "I hope you break your neck."'

'Have they taken in Gervase Hart?'

'No, not him.'

'I wonder why. He was overheard telling Penelope he'd kill her.'

'Who told you that?' demanded Fiona sharply.

'Meaning you've told them all to shut up, except when it comes to Sheila.'

'That's not the case at all.'

Hamish sighed. 'Lies, lies and more lies. Don't go around trying to hide things from the police. All it means is that a lot of innocent people get grilled by Blair when the murderer could be running around loose.'

He decided to spend what was left of the day trying to find out if anyone had seen Patricia on the morning of the murder. He drove over to Golspie and learned that the police had already questioned the waitresses at the Sutherland Arms Hotel and had found that Patricia did indeed have lunch there. No one had noticed that her manner was anything out of the way. She had, for example, not been muttering and talking to herself as she had been on the day that Dr Brodie had found her. But although he diligently checked around Golspie – calling first on Hugh Johnston, the owner of Golspie Motors, the main garage – no one had seen Patricia or her car. It was a white Metro. Perhaps she had stopped somewhere for petrol. He drove miles, checking at petrol stations without success.

\* \* \*

Colin Jessop, the minister, arrived back at the manse and called, 'Eileen!' No one answered. He went through to the kitchen. There was a note on the kitchen counter. It read, 'Gone to Inverness with Ailsa. If I am not back, there is a casserole of stew in the fridge. Just heat it for your dinner.'

He glared at the note and then crumpled it into a ball. It was this silly film business of Eileen's that was making her forget her duties as a wife. Well, as soon as she got back, he would put a stop to it.

He ate his solitary dinner, looking all the time at the kitchen clock. At nine o'clock he heard a car drive up.

He got to his feet.

His wife came in. He stared at her in outrage, at her make-up and at her dyed hair.

'You look a disgrace,' he shouted, the veins standing out on his forehead. 'You will go and wash that muck off your face, and tomorrow you will get your hair put back to normal, and then you will stop this film business which is leading you into the paths of sin.'

Eileen looked at him coolly. 'At least my hair is not bleached blonde. I was in that new restaurant in Inverness today. What's it called? I know. Harry's. That's the place. You see some interesting sights in there. I wonder what your parishioners would say if I described one of the sights I saw. But I'll say no more about it,

181

Colin. The hair stays, the make-up stays and the filming goes on.'

He sank down slowly into his chair. Eileen gave him a gentle smile and went out, quietly closing the kitchen door behind her.


Hamish sat in front of the computer that evening. He tried Blair's password again, fully expecting to find it had been changed; but unlike before, for some reason, his hacking had not yet been discovered.

He studied the reports.

Fiona King said she had backed off a little because she wanted a cigarette and Giles Brown, the director, couldn't bear the smell of cigarette smoke. Gervase Hart said that he was bored and had strolled off a bit, looking for somewhere to sit down. Sheila said she had shown Penelope where to stand and then had gone back to join the others. Giles Brown confirmed that Sheila had been beside him when Penelope had screamed, so she could not possibly have done it. Harry Frame said he had gone off to find a quiet place in the mist for a pee. Patricia kept to her story about driving mindlessly around. No, she had not stopped for petrol. She had had a full tank when she set out.

Hamish ploughed on through all the reports from various members of the television company, from the estate staff at Drim Castle, from the villagers of Drim.

He sat back, bewildered.

Who on earth could have murdered Penelope?

The clue to it must lie somewhere in her background, and that background lay in Glasgow.

He picked up the phone and called Detective Sergeant Bill Walton of the Glasgow police, an old friend. He was told Walton was off duty that day, so he called his home number.

'So it's you, Hamish,' said Bill cheerfully. 'My, you do have exotic murders up there. All we've got here is pedestrian jobs like slashings, muggings and drugs. No beautiful actresses.'

'It's this Penelope Gates, Bill,' said Hamish. 'It's a mess.' He outlined the suspects. 'You see what I mean?' he said finally. 'Any of them could have done it. It was a simple murder where someone saw an opportunity of getting rid of her. I don't think it was planned. So I was wondering if you had been on the case, if there was anything in Penelope's background.'

'I've been working on it a bit,' said Bill, 'and yes, I've been digging into Penelope's background. She comes from a pretty slummy home in Parkhead.'

'And how did she manage to get to the Royal Academy of Dramatic Art?'

'That was the mother. Saw her daughter as a modern Shirley Temple, always putting her into children's competitions, all curls and frilly dresses. Got the money out of a doting uncle who keeps a newsagent's in Cumbernauld. Violent, bullying father, minor offences, drunk and disorderly mostly.'

'Any boyfriends in the past?'

'I gather mother kept her under wraps and was furious when she married Josh. Would guess our Penelope was a virgin until she married Josh, unless that uncle she hated meddled with her. He was suspected at one time of child abuse, but nothing was ever proved.'

'Could be that uncle. She could have threatened to expose him.'

'Uncle was on holiday in Tenerife when the murder happened. I saw that writer woman on television. My money's on her.'

'Why?'

'She came across as arrogant as sin and as cold as hell.'

'She's quite vulnerable,' said Hamish slowly. 'In fact, she offered to pay me to find out who really did it.'

'Could have done that to throw you off the scent.'

'Don't think so,' said Hamish with a flash of arrogance. 'I do haff the reputation up here.'

'Okay, Sherlock, but I don't think I can help you.'

'There's another thing. That death of Jamie Gallagher. I've got a feeling in my bones that Josh didn't do it.'

'So just suppose for a minute you're right. Who would want to get rid of both Jamie and Penelope?'

'Fiona King,' said Hamish. 'The producer. She's a hard-bitten, pot-smoking woman, and her job was under threat from both of them.'

'Could she have killed Penelope? She was on the wrong side of the camera, if you know what I mean.'

'She could have sprinted off through the mist. The mist and the heather block out sound.' He described the outcrop and the little space underneath.

'But no matter how thick the mist, Penelope would have seen her or at least heard her.'

'I thought of that, but she could have muttered something like "Just checking", slid over the edge and waited.'

'You're making my head ache, Hamish, but if anything comes up, I'll let you know.'

Hamish said goodbye and rang off.

Almost immediately the phone rang. It was Jimmy Anderson.

'Just thought you would like to know,' he said, 'Patricia Martyn-Broyd collapsed under Blair's grilling and was taken off to hospital in Strathbane. Posse of lawyers from the TV company moved in. Police harassment and all that. Blair is in deep shit.'

'I'll go and see her. Aren't you coming for your whisky?'

'Can't get away.'

'I'll drop in and see you after I've seen Patricia.'

'Patricia, is it. Quite matey, are you?'

'Love her to death,' said Hamish.

He said goodbye to Jimmy and went out and got into the police Land Rover. As he drove along the waterfront, he saw with a sort of amazement that Lochdubh, tranquil in the evening light, looked the same. The fishing boats were chugging out down the sea loch from the harbour, children played on the shingly beach, the mountains soared up into the clear air and people were coming and going from Patel's shop, which stayed open late.

He reached the hump-backed bridge which spanned the road leading out of Lochdubh and then put his foot down on the accelerator and sped towards Strathbane.

It was only when he was halfway there that he remembered he had not delivered the fish to Angus. The Highland part of him hoped the seer would not zap him with something bad, but the commonsense side told himself severely that such a fear was ridiculous.

# Chapter Seven

*I hope I shall never be deterred from detecting
what I think a cheat, by the menaces of a ruffian.*
                              – Dr Samuel Johnson

A woman police constable was on duty outside Patricia's hospital room. 'She's sleeping,'
she told Hamish when he arrived. 'They gave
her a sedative.'

'What was she like when she was brought
in?' asked Hamish.

'Weeping and mumbling.'

'I'll go in and sit with her for a bit.'

The policewoman sat down again and
flipped open the magazine she had been reading. 'Suit yourself. But I don't think she'll
wake up for ages.'

Hamish went in. Patricia Martyn-Broyd
looked very small and frail under the bed-
clothes. Her face had a waxen pallor. Damn
Blair, thought Hamish, he's gone too far this
time.

He pulled up a chair and sat down by the bed and looked around. It was the usual sterile hospital room. No flowers or cards, of course. Poor Patricia.

She stirred and mumbled in her sleep. Hamish leaned forward. He felt he should let her sleep on but on the other hand did not want to return to Lochdubh without having found something out.

'Patricia!' he said urgently.

She mumbled again, and then her eyes opened. She looked around in a dazed way.

'You are in the hospital in Strathbane,' said Hamish.

'What happened?' she said weakly. 'Did I have an accident?'

'No, you collapsed while you were being interviewed by Detective Chief Inspector Blair.'

'Who is he? Who are you?' demanded Patricia, her eyes frightened.

'It iss me,' said Hamish anxiously. 'Hamish Macbeth.'

'I can't remember,' she said weakly.

'The murder,' he said urgently.

'What murder? What are you talking about?' Her thin hands began to claw the sheet.

Hamish went out into the corridor. 'You'd better get a doctor,' he said to the police-woman. 'She's in a fair state and cannae remember a thing.'

A doctor and a nurse were summoned and hurried into the room, firmly shutting Hamish outside.

Hamish and the policewoman waited in silence. Finally the doctor emerged. 'I've given her another sedative, and the hospital psychiatrist will see her in the morning. She needs absolute quiet and rest. I've read in the newspapers about bullying police tactics and never believed them until now. It's a disgrace!'

Hamish went off to police headquarters in Strathbane. He met Superintendent Peter Daviot as he was going into the building. 'Well, Hamish?' said Daviot. 'Any news?'

'I called at the hospital to see Miss Martyn-Broyd,' said Hamish. 'She is in a bad state of shock and appears to have lost her memory.'

'This is dreadful.' Daviot turned and walked with Hamish back into the building. 'Blair will need to be suspended, pending a full enquiry.'

'And who will take over the case, sir? Jimmy Anderson?'

'No, we need someone senior. I've already called Detective Chief Inspector Lovelace of Inverness to head the investigations.'

'And what's he like?' asked Hamish, thinking that Lovelace sounded a friendly sort of name.

'He is a competent officer, and that is all you need to know, Macbeth.'

Hamish went into the CID room. Through the usual haze of smoke he could see Jimmy Anderson, sitting at his desk.

'Keeping that Scotch warm for me, Hamish?'

'Aye, it's there for you when you want a dram. Blair's been suspended. I've just seen Daviot.'

'Man, that's great. My chance for glory.'

'Sorry, Jimmy. He's putting some man, Lovelace, from Inverness, in charge.'

Jimmy's face darkened. 'A new man will need to begin at the beginning. I don't like Blair, but he's the evil I know, if you get me.'

'I've just come from the hospital,' said Hamish. 'Patricia's in a right taking. Lost her memory.'

'How convenient,' sneered Jimmy.

'If she's putting it on, she's a better actress than I would ha' guessed,' said Hamish. 'I cannae help feeling we're looking at all this the wrong way round. Now, just supposing Josh Gates didn't murder Jamie Gallagher and the person who really murdered Jamie murdered Penelope, who would spring to mind?'

'Thon producer woman. Hard as nails. You could strike matches on her bum.'

'Apart from her.'

Jimmy scowled horribly. Then he said, 'If they were both such a threat to the success of the TV thing, then there's Harry Frame.'

'So there is. I might call on him.'

Jimmy looked up at the clock on the wall through the fog of cigarette smoke. 'It's eleven o'clock at night, man!'

'I bet they're all still awake. I'll take my chances.'

Hamish found Harry Frame in the bar of the Tommel Castle Hotel. The big man was alone and slumped over a pint of beer.

'More police,' he said when he saw Hamish. 'Haven't you lot done enough? Poor old Patricia.'

'I thought you lot considered her a pain in the neck.'

'No one should suffer a breakdown because of police harassment,' said Harry truculently. 'That man Blair!'

'Well, he's off the case. What I am curious about is whether you believe that Josh Gates killed Jamie Gallagher.'

'For heaven's sake, it's nearly midnight and I am being kept up by the daft notions of the village bobby. I shouldn't have to tell you your job. Josh was found with Jamie's blood on his hands.'

'Aye, but to my reckoning, Josh could have found the body, raised the head to see if he was dead, got blood on his hands and ran away in a panic and got drunk for the last time. Jamie was sabotaging the series with his interference and his dull scripts. Yes, I bet they were dull, and I bet when Angus Harris turned up claiming Jamie had stolen the script of *Football Fever*, you believed him. And Penelope

Gates was starting to act like a prima donna and wanted everyone fired.'

Harry Frame stood up and loomed over Hamish. 'You lot are in deep shit. You've driven Patricia into a nervous breakdown. And now you, a village copper, are threatening me.'

'I never did.'

'Oh, yes, you are hinting with the subtlety of an ox that I murdered both Penelope and Jamie. Your superiors will hear about this.'

Harry stormed off. Hamish looked after him curiously and then gave a shrug.

The big man could complain all he wanted. All Hamish had done was have a chat with him. Nothing would come of it.

In this, Hamish Macbeth was wrong.

The following morning, before Hamish had had time to change into his uniform and while he was repairing a broken plank on his henhouse, Detective Chief Inspector Lovelace arrived.

Flanked by Detectives Anderson and Macnab, he stood watching Hamish until Hamish, aware of his gaze, turned round.

Lovelace introduced himself and then said curtly, 'May we go inside? Anderson and Macnab, wait here.'

They walked indoors to the police station. Lovelace sat behind Hamish's desk and folded a pair of white, well-manicured hands on the desk in front of him. Hamish stood before him.

Lovelace was a small, neat man with well-brushed fair hair. He had neat features and a small, prissy mouth. He looked at a corner of the ceiling and began. Hamish was to learn that Lovelace never looked you in the eye, not out of shyness or furtiveness, but more as if he thought his august gaze was too valuable to waste on underlings.

'We will begin by asking why you are not in uniform.'

'I wass chust attending to a few chores.'

'To a few chores . . . what?'

'To a few chores, sir.'

'You are being paid to police Lochdubh and the surrounding area, not to repair henhouses. Why did you call on Patricia Martyn-Broyd at the hospital without telling your superiors what you were doing and why?'

'I know Miss Martyn-Broyd. I mean, I have known her since before the murders. We are by way of being friends,' lied Hamish. He did not want to tell Lovelace that Patricia had asked him to find out the identity of the murderer.

'Nonetheless, it was your duty to inform your superiors of your movements. To the even more serious matter. You bullied and harassed Mr Harry Frame last night and accused him of being a double murderer.'

'I did not . . . sir. I was merely interested in discussing my views with him.'

Lovelace's gaze shifted to the window. There was a long silence.

A child shrieked, 'Gie that back, Hughie!' somewhere out on the waterfront, a dog barked and a wind sighed down the loch.

'I have heard of your way of doing things,' said Lovelace at last. 'This is not the Wild West and you are not an American sheriff. You will not step out of line again, and in order to make sure that you do not, I am giving you these orders. You will confine yourself to your duties as a village constable. I am now in charge of the murder inquiry. There are enough people working under me to deal with it. Do not approach anyone concerned with the case.'

He stood up and walked to the door. Then he swung round. 'And get your uniform on!'

After he had heard him drive off, Hamish slumped down behind his desk. He was, he thought miserably, not suited for the police force. He enjoyed his job until he ran up against the pecking order of the British police force. Except during a major case like this, he was usually left to his own devices.

Now he could not dare go near Drim, or see Sheila, and right at that moment, he would have liked to see Sheila. She was not only pretty, there was an endearing warmth about her.

Gloomily judging that he would not have to sustain another visit that day from Lovelace, he went back to repairing the henhouse and when that job was finished, he got the trout out of the freezer and strolled along the waterfront and up the hill to the seer's cottage.

'Took your time,' said Angus by way of greeting. 'So they've driven that poor woman mad, have they?'

'How did you find out so quickly?'

Angus tapped his forehead and winked, and Hamish looked at him impatiently. 'I wish I had your network of gossip, Angus, because I'm off the case.'

'What's the new man like?'

'So you even know there's a new man? Oh, don't tap your forehead again. He's a pompous little fart,' said Hamish bitterly. 'He called on me this morning.'

'And you not even in uniform. My, my.'

Hamish's eyes fell on an expensive basket of fruit on the table. He jerked a thumb at it. 'What's that for? Going hospital visiting?'

'That iss the present from a grateful client. They are not all as mean as Hamish Macbeth.'

'Any of the TV people come to see you?'

'That would be telling. I neffer betray the confidences of my clients.'

'Then I won't waste any more time with you,' said Hamish, going to the door.

Angus followed him. 'I warned you not to get your hopes up about that wee blonde lassie.'

'I don't see much hope of that,' retorted Hamish. 'I've been told to keep clear, so I probably won't see her again.'

'Not unless you hurry.'

'What are you talking about?'

'Herself has chust driven up to the police station.'

Hamish stared down the hillside. A car had driven up outside the police station, and he could see the glint of blonde hair as the driver got out.

He muttered an exclamation and began to run off down the hill, his long legs going like pistons.

As he arrived at the police station, Sheila was just driving off. He waved and shouted, and she screeched to a halt and then turned the car and headed back in his direction.

'Hello, Hamish,' she said, getting out of the car again. She was wearing a shirt blouse, shorts and sandals. Her legs were muscular but well shaped, smooth and tanned.

'Come in and have a coffee,' panted Hamish.

'Where did you come from?' Sheila asked.

'I wass up seeing Angus Macdonald, the seer.'

'I've heard of him. Any good?'

'Nothing but an old gossip,' said Hamish, leading the way into the kitchen. 'Coffee?' He plugged in the electric kettle.

'That would be nice,' said Sheila. 'I didn't know you had gone modern.'

'What?'

'The electric kettle. I thought you had to

196

light that stove every time you wanted a cup of tea.'

'Och, no, I only use it for cooking. Milk and sugar?'

She nodded.

'So what brings you?'

'I've got a break. There's to be no filming today. The lawyers are locked in battle with the police. But the police have a statement from the people in Drim that Patricia had already gone potty, so they might not get very far. I thought you'd be over with them.'

'I've been taken off the case by the new man.'

'Do you find that hard?'

'Yes, I do. These murders took place on my beat. I know all the locals. I should not have been left out. How are things in Drim?'

'Seething. It's a funny place. When we first arrived, I thought it was lovely, a sort of Brigadoon, leisurely and kind. But after a bit, I got to know some of the locals that are being used as extras. They can be quite spiteful about each other. Edie Aubrey, that thin woman who does the exercise classes, got one line to say, that was all, and the other women ganged up and said unless they had something to say themselves, they wouldn't appear. Fiona told them that the whole thing would go on without them and they backed down, but none of them are speaking to Edie, and someone threw a brick through her living room window.'

'That's Drim for you.'

'And Alice, the hairdresser, she also had a line to say. Now, she had an extra bathroom put in upstairs two years ago, and she never bothered getting planning permission for it, and suddenly someone reports the existence of that bathroom to the council and she's in trouble. And yet they all seemed like such friends.'

'It's a closed-down sort of place, cut off by the mountains and the loch,' said Hamish, 'and the winters up here are long and dark. They've nothing else to do but study each other.'

'I thought watching television would have given them a broader outlook.'

'It narrowed it. They watch the soaps, you see, and that turns them into drama queens. One of the women confided in me last year that she had low self-esteem because her mother never said she loved her. A Scottish mother, for heaven's sake, does not go about telling her children she loves them. It is just something up here that's expected to be understood. Then those American chat shows are a curse. I 'member when a few of the biddies decided they had been sexually abused in their youth.'

'I thought there might be a lot of incest in these villages.'

'Not with the church being so strong. They'd be affeard that God would strike them dead. Anyway, it seems as if no one is ever going to find out what happened to Penelope. Do you know that Harry Frame reported me to my superiors for harassment?'

'Yes, he was fuming about that this morning. Do you think he did it? Come on, Hamish! Harry!'

'Chust a thought,' said Hamish huffily, because he was privately wishing he had never approached Harry Frame.

'I mean, why?'

'Because Jamie was buggering up the film and then Penelope. Will it run smoothly with both of them out the way?'

'Well, yes. Mary Hoyle is a very good actress. And she never throws scenes, she doesn't drink and she has a reputation of never being late on the set and of taking direction. She's a director's dream.'

'Giles Brown is the director.'

'Don't get any ideas there. He couldn't hurt a rabbit. In fact, he is a bit of a rabbit.'

'Would you like to go out for dinner tonight?' asked Hamish.

'That would be nice. Where?'

'The Napoli.'

'Is nine o'clock too late?'

'No, that'll be just fine.'

Sheila rose. 'See you then, copper.'

Hamish admired her sturdy legs as she walked out of the kitchen. Sheila got in the car and drove slowly off. Then she stopped outside the general store, went in and asked where the seer lived.

Having got directions, she drove up to the back of the village and parked the car at the bottom of the long winding path which led up to Angus's cottage. She had bought a bottle of wine in Patel's since she had heard the seer expected a gift.

Despite her natural cynicism, she was impressed with Angus's old cottage and by Angus himself, with his long beard and piercing eyes.

'So,' said Angus after they were seated, 'it iss the famous Miss Sheila Burford.'

'How do you know my name?'

Angus smiled at her. 'I see everything.'

'I am not famous. You are mistaken about that. I am a combination of researcher, secretary, office girl, tea maker and general dogsbody. Strathclyde Television does that soap *The Highland Way*. Harry promised me I could direct one of the episodes, but nothing's come of it.'

'I see it all. You won't be a director.'

'I thought that,' said Sheila gloomily.

'You'll make your name as a producer.'

'I don't think so.'

'I am neffer wrong. So you are wasting your time thinking about marriage.'

'Doesn't every girl?'

'A pretty young thing like yourself, with all that ambition inside you, should not be contemplating throwing her career away by getting married to a village policeman.'

Sheila coloured but laughed. 'Hamish and I are just friends.'

'Remember what I said,' intoned Angus. 'Now I am tired. The spirits have left me.'

'I didn't even know they had arrived,' said Sheila, getting to her feet. She waited a moment to see if he had anything more to say, but the seer had lain back in his chair and closed his eyes.

Sheila made her way thoughtfully down the path to her car. It was all a load of rubbish, of course. Still, it would do no harm to seek out Harry Frame if he had not left for Glasgow and tackle him about that director's job.

When she got back to Drim, it was to find Harry closeted with the lawyers. It was late afternoon before he emerged from the room in which they had been holding their meeting.

'Can I have a word with you, Harry?' asked Sheila.

'Just a few minutes. I have to get down to Glasgow. We'll use Fiona's office. It's empty at the moment.'

They went inside and Harry closed the door.

'It's like this,' said Sheila. 'You know I work hard.'

'None better,' said Harry. His eyes fell to her legs. Sheila tucked them under her chair.

'You've been saying for ages that I could direct an episode of *The Highland Way*. Any chance of that?'

He was sitting opposite her. He drew his chair closer until their knees were almost touching.

'Your work for me is appreciated, Sheila. You know that. You're a pretty girl and we get on fine. In fact, we could get on better.' He put a large hand on her knee and squeezed it.

'Harry,' said Sheila, 'I would like that director's job because you think I can do it and not for any other reason.'

'No, no,' he said, caressing her knee. 'But I could be of great help to you in your career.' The hand left her knee and clasped her breast.

She jerked away and stood up. 'Forget it, Harry,' she said, and went quickly out of the room.

She ran through the castle and out into the courtyard. Damn that seer. She was not going on anyone's casting couch.


Eileen Jessop gathered up her cartridges of videotape. She needed help, and now that Colin was not going to stand in her way, she was going to go to Drim Castle and ask Fiona King if she might have time to look at some of the film and see if someone could help her edit it.

Wearing make-up and her new shirtwaister dress, she drove to the castle. The first person she saw in the courtyard was Sheila.

'It is Miss Burford, is it not?' asked Eileen, suddenly feeling dowdy before this picture of glowing youth.

Sheila did not recognize the minister's wife.

'I am Eileen Jessop. We met when you were looking for a location. I am the minister's wife.'

'Oh, yes, I remember you now,' said Sheila politely, although her mind was still filled with outrage at Harry's advances. She felt in her bones that once the series was filmed he would get rid of her as soon as he could.

'I wonder if I might see Miss Fiona King. I wanted her help in a little matter.'

'She wasn't in her office,' began Sheila, and then she saw Fiona striding into the courtyard. 'There she is now. Fiona!'

Fiona joined them. 'This is Eileen Jessop, the minister's wife,' said Sheila.

'Oh, yes,' said Fiona, looking edgy and harassed. It had been a long day.

Eileen surveyed her timidly and then took a deep breath. 'I have been filming a play of mine, using the village women as actresses. The film needs cutting and editing. I wondered if you could spare the time to see a little of it, and perhaps one of your staff could advise me.'

Fiona was usually tactful, but the stress of the murders and the police investigation into Penelope's murder had shredded her nerves. All she wanted was a deep bath and a cold drink.

'We are a professional television company,' she said nastily, 'and you should know we hardly have time to break off our work to cope with amateur dramatics. I am sorry, but that's the way it is. Sheila, I'll be at the hotel if anyone wants me.'

She strode off.

Sheila saw that Eileen was red with mortification. She looked at her watch. 'I'm meeting someone for dinner, but I've an hour to spare. Bring your stuff and I'll look at it for you.'

'I feel ashamed of myself now,' said Eileen, clutching her cartridges protectively to her chest. 'You'll just be bored.'

Probably to death, thought Sheila. But she was sorry for the minister's wife, so she said instead, 'Come along. I'm dying to see it.'

She led the way to Fiona's office, pushing open the door cautiously in case Harry Frame should still be there, but to her relief the room was empty.

'This is the first one,' said Eileen eagerly, handing her a cartridge.

At least I've got that dinner date with Hamish as an excuse not to stay too long, thought Sheila, repressing a sigh.

She sat back and began watch. Then she leaned forward a little in her seat. To Eileen it was agony, for Sheila made no comment. She went through cartridge after cartridge. The black hands on the face of the large clock on the wall moved up to nine o'clock and on past, and still Sheila watched.

Sheila felt the palms of her hands damp with excitement. What a gem! The script was witty and funny. The village women were natural actresses, and there were miles of tape where the bad camera angles and occasional fluffed lines could be cut.

At last Sheila said, 'Have you shown this to anyone else?'

'I've shown it to the village women, of course.'

'But to no one else on the television company?'

'No.'

Sheila took a deep breath. 'I'll tell you what I'll do. Leave this with me to cut and edit. I will then try to sell it to a television company if you let me put my name on it as producer and we share the profits – thirty percent to me, and the rest to you.'

Eileen's voice trembled. 'Do you mean you like it?'

'It's marvellous. Very clever. I haven't seen anything so innocently funny since *Whisky Galore*. But you must keep very quiet about it.'

'Oh, I will. I won't even tell my husband.'
'Okay, let's just go through it again.'


Hamish Macbeth gloomily finished his solitary meal in the Napoli. She could have got tied up with something, but the place over there was crawling with mobile phones. She could at least have phoned. He had been rejected all round, off the case, and stood up by Sheila.

But there was still something he could do for Patricia in his spare time. Somehow, somewhere, he would find someone who had seen her on the day of the murder.


Eileen Jessop left Drim Castle after midnight, her eyes shining and her face flushed. That drive to Inverness with Ailsa had changed her life. She longed to tell Ailsa about what Sheila had said of the film, but she had promised Sheila not to breathe a word. She remembered all Sheila's advice and comments. She would get all the women together and try again, making it glossier and sharper. Sheila had said that was not necessary, but it would give them all something to do while she waited to see if Sheila could sell the film.

As she approached the grim bulk of the manse, her heart sank. And then for the first time she wondered why she stayed married to Colin. She could just get in the car and drive away into the sunshine as she had driven down to Inverness with Ailsa, with the wind in her hair and the tape deck blasting.

The next day Hamish put on his uniform and went out on his rounds. He had a feeling that Lovelace might call at the police station to make sure he was not slacking off. He drove over to Cnothan and started again to ask questions. The trouble was that Patricia's cottage was outside the village and she did not need to drive through Cnothan to get anywhere.

He started at one end of the village and began knocking on doors, patiently questioning without success.

Cnothan stood on the edge of an artificial loch caused by an ugly hydro electric dam. It consisted of one bleak main street which led down to the loch. The council houses were segregated on the other side of the loch from the main village, but the privately owned houses in the village were so drab and grey that they looked like the council ones. The people of Cnothan seemed to have been soured by their surroundings. All he got were curt, rude answers. The villagers had a capacity for making work. They were always rushing about doing nothing. 'I'm too busy to speak to you,' seemed to be the standard reply.

In his zeal to find out where Patricia had been, he had quite forgotten he was poaching on Sergeant MacGregor's territory until, on leaving one house at the top of the main street, he found the sergeant standing by the garden gate, glaring at him.

'Whit are you doing here?' demanded the sergeant.

'Can we go somewhere and talk?'

'Aye, come up to the house until we sort this thing out.'

Hamish thought Sergeant MacGregor's house reflected everything that was worst about Cnothan. Even on this summer's day, it felt cold.

The living room was still the same as the last time he had seen it, with its dreadful ornaments and overstuffed salmon-coloured three-piece suite.

'Now what's this all about?' demanded Sergeant MacGregor.

'It's like this,' said Hamish. 'I have a quiet day today and I thought I might find out if anyone had seen Patricia Martyn-Broyd on the day of the murder. I should have called you first, but I did not think you would be wanting to waste your time with this sort of inquiry. In fact, I have to beg you not to report my visit here.'

'Why?'

'Blair has been suspended and Lovelace is in charge of the case, and he told me to butt out.'

'Lovelace!' MacGregor's face darkened. 'Thon bastard.'

'You know him?'

'Know him? I was off duty in Inverness five years ago and I nipped into a pub for a drink before I got home. I didn't know Lovelace, so I didn't recognize him. I got talking to a crony, had a few more. When I left the pub and got in the car, Lovelace and two coppers were waiting to breathalyze me. He insisted on putting in a report, and I nearly lost my job. If that's all you're doing in Cnothan, you can go ahead. He won't be hearing anything from me.'

'That's good of you,' said Hamish with relief. Lovelace could certainly have handled that affair better. He could have strolled over to MacGregor in the bar and introduced himself, and MacGregor would have been out of there like a shot. Of course, it could be argued that MacGregor should not have been taking one nip over the limit, but still, it seemed an unnecessarily harsh way of doing things.

'Have you any idea where I might find out something about where our writer went that day, the day Penelope Gates was murdered?' asked Hamish.

'Haven't a clue. Wait a minute. There might be the one person.'

'Who?'

'Sean Fitz is back on the road.'

Sean Fitzpatrick, known all over the Highlands as simply Sean Fitz, was an itinerant tramp, calling at doors to do small jobs in return for a cup of tea and a bite of food.

No one had seen him for the past two years.

'Where has he been?' asked Hamish.

'Don't know. Maybe down south. But he's your man.'

Hamish thanked him and set out to try to find Sean. Sean Fitz noticed everything and everybody on the road.

# Chapter Eight

*They flee from me, that sometime did me seek.*
— Sir Thomas Wyatt

Two days later, a good number of the village women who had acted in Eileen's film were gathered in the manse.

For the first time, Eileen became aware that there was a sour atmosphere. Nonetheless she was determined that nothing was going to take the glow out of her achievement, even though she could not talk about it.

She stood up before them and cleared her throat. 'There are a few mistakes in act one that need to be fixed. I thought we could film it again.'

There was an impatient, restless shuffling. Then Nancy Macleod stood up. 'We cannae really be wasting any more time on your fillum, Mrs Jessop. We've got other things to do.'

Eileen looked at her in surprise.

'You see,' said Holly Andrews, Ailsa's friend, whose nose had been put out of joint because of the friendship which had grown up between Ailsa and the minister's wife, 'we all feel we're wasting our time with an amateur film when we're in the real thing.'

'But you are only in several of the crowd scenes in *The Case of the Rising Tides*,' protested Eileen.

'But Edie Aubrey got a speaking part,' said Nancy. 'There's a chance for us all tae be discovered.'

'Where is Edie?' asked Eileen. 'And shouldn't Alice be here as well?'

A hostile silence greeted her.

'So we'd best all be going,' said Nancy.

Eileen watched them all, with the exception of Ailsa, depart in silence.

As soon as she was alone with Ailsa, she asked, 'What has gone wrong? Up till now they've all enjoyed acting for me. They said they'd never had so much fun.'

'They've been discontented for some time,' said Ailsa.

'I didn't know that!'

'It's because you're the minister's wife. It's like that in Highland villages with the minister's wife. They're usually respectful.'

'Why didn't you tell me?'

'You were enjoying yourself. No need to involve you in squabbles. But Edie Aubrey got a chance to say one line and so someone threw a brick through her front window.'

'Who did it? What did the police say?'

'Edie never reported it. We police ourselves here.'

'They cannot possibly think they are going to be film stars!'

'That's exactly what the silly biddies do think. Cheer up. You've got masses of film already.'

'But I could still have done better,' wailed Eileen.

'Never mind. You've lost weight.'

'I've been on a diet,' said Eileen in an abstracted way. 'I should do something about this. Why should some jealous woman get away with terrorizing poor Edie?'

'It'll all blow over, you'll see,' said Ailsa. 'Now I'd better get back and take over from Jock and mind the store. He's got a shinty game over in Crask this afternoon.'

After she had gone, Eileen paced up and down. Then she came to a decision, got in her car and drove over to Lochdubh and parked outside the police station.

Hamish was feeling tired. In between his other duties, he had driven all over the place, searching for Sean Fitz. If only the morning of the murder hadn't been thick with mist.

He opened the door to Eileen and looked at her in polite inquiry, not recognizing the minister's wife in the slimmer, dark-haired woman who stood blinking myopically up at him.

'We met before,' she said, holding out her hand. 'I am Eileen Jessop, the minister's wife . . . at Drim, that is. You called on myself and my husband shortly after we moved up here.'

'So I did. Come in. Tea? Coffee?'

'Coffee would be nice,' said Eileen.

'Then pull up a chair.'

Eileen sat down at the kitchen table. Then she said, 'Perhaps I should be telling you this in the police office. It's a police matter.'

'You can tell me just the same over a cup of coffee.' He plugged in the kettle and took down two mugs and a bowl of sugar and took a jug of milk out of the fridge. Eileen waited until he had handed her a mug of coffee and sat down.

'Now,' said Hamish, 'what is this all about?'

He was really a very attractive man, thought Eileen, and her next thought was that it was a long time since she had really looked at any man to find him attractive or otherwise.

'It's this TV film. It's causing bad feeling among the village women. Now it's turned criminal. Edie Aubrey got a line to say instead of just being in the crowd scene like the others and so someone threw a brick through her window.'

'Well, that's Drim for you.'

'But they were not like this before!'

'They have been,' said Hamish, remembering that murder case a few years before. 'If it is any comfort to you, tempers flare among

214

them, but if you try to interfere, they close ranks against you.'

'But you must do something!'

Hamish was about to say if Edie had not reported it, there was little he could do; but suddenly he saw a great way of being officially back in Drim.

'Wait until you've finished your coffee and then I'll follow you over and see if I can do something to frighten them into good behaviour. So how are you getting on? I heard something about you making a film.'

'Oh, it's just a silly little thing,' said Eileen, who had become increasingly depressed about her play on the way over. She had even begun to worry that Sheila had just been humouring her. 'But it was fun while it lasted.'

'What's it about, your film?'

'I wrote a Scottish play when I was a student. It's comedy with a dark side. It's about an eccentric woman who arrives to live in a small Highland village and gets damned as being a witch. I changed the title to *The Witch of Drim*. I would have liked to do some more work on it, but the village women have decided they do not want to be involved in amateur dramatics any more.'

'I suppose they think that Spielberg or someone will see their unlovely faces on the Strathclyde Television thing and say, "That's the woman for me!"'

'That is just what they are thinking.'

'Don't worry. I'll do something. Is Drim still full of the press?'

'They've mostly gone. I believe some of the nationals have left a few reporters up here, but they are down in Strathbane. There's some scandal about poor Miss Martyn-Broyd being driven into a nervous breakdown.'

'Is that young lassie Sheila Burford around? She was supposed to meet me for dinner on Monday and she didn't turn up or even bother to phone.'

Monday, thought Eileen. Monday was when she had seen Sheila. And Sheila had forgotten her date with this attractive policeman to look at her, Eileen's, film. Her heart soared and she gave Hamish a radiant smile. Then she said, 'I asked for her at the castle before I came here. She said she had to go down to Glasgow for a funeral.'

Hamish hoped against hope that bad news had made her forget their date. He did not like to think he had not been worth even a phone call.

Eileen finished her coffee, thanked Hamish and left. Hamish washed out the cups, put the milk back in the fridge, locked up the police station and got into the police Land Rover and took the winding road to Drim.

There was no filming that day, and Drim lay peacefully in the sunshine, as if murder had never taken place.

He parked the Land Rover outside the general store and then walked to Edie Aubrey's cottage. The front window was boarded up. In a more civilized part of the country, a glazier would have replaced the broken window by now, but in the Highlands it was very hard to get anything repaired quickly. Glaziers, plumbers, electricians, men who repaired dry stone walls and builders all seemed to suffer from bad backs. The work always eventually got done, but it took a long time.

He knocked on the door, and after a few moments Edie answered it. She was a scrawny woman with thick glasses and dressed in a track suit of a violent shade of red.

'Hamish!' she said. 'What brings you?'

'Can I come in?'

'Yes, of course. I was just about to put the kettle on. Take a seat in the lounge.'

Hamish went into an uncomfortable, over-decorated room. Although not a Highlander, Edie had adopted the Highland way of keeping one room for 'best', so it had that clean, glittering look and stuffy, unused smell. It was all in shades of pink. Barbara Cartland would have loved it. There was a pink three-piece suite upholstered in some nasty slippery material. Pink curtains hung at the boarded-up window, and the walls were painted in a shade Hamish recognized as being called blush pink. Pink scatter cushions cascaded on to the floor as he sat down. The sofa was so overstuffed, he felt himself slipping forwards, so he retrieved the cushions and then sat down on the one hard upright chair in the room.

Edie came in carrying a glass tray with thin cups on it, cups embellished with gold rims and pink roses.

'Could we have some light in here, Edie?' asked Hamish, peering at her through the gloom.

'Of course.' She switched on a pink-shaded, pink-fringed standard lamp.

'Now, Edie, what happened to your window?'

'The silliest thing,' said Edie with awful brightness. 'I was vacuuming the room and I slipped and the end of the vacuum went straight through the window.'

'So all this talk about someone throwing a brick through the window is lies? Come on, Edie, I'm not daft and I know what goes on in Drim. Someone was jealous of you getting a wee speaking part.'

Edie glared at him and then shrugged her thin shoulders. 'Oh, well, you know how we are here. Someone pushed money in an envelope through the letter box the other day for the repairs. We settle our own disputes.'

'You are a bunch of silly hens,' said Hamish. 'And what about this film the minister's wife is doing?'

'Oh, that was fun for a while,' said Edie, lying back against the sofa in a jaded, sophisticated way. 'But we can't be caught up in the wee woman's amateur dramatics every day of the week.'

'You're making a big mistake there,' said Hamish. 'Oh, me and my big mouth!'

Edie sat up straight. 'What do you know?'

Hamish smiled at her ruefully and then shrugged. 'Oh, well, then I'll tell ye, Edie, but it's to be a secret, chust between the two of us. Promise you won't breathe a word!'

'I promise. Would you like a dram?'

'No, it's too early and I'm driving.' He leaned forward and lowered his voice. 'As part of this murder case, I haff been checking up on the backgrounds of everyone.'

'I heard you were off it,' said Edie.

'This was afore,' said Hamish huffily. 'Do you want to hear this or not?'

'Yes, yes, go on.'

Hamish took a slow sip of tea while Edie waited eagerly.

'In the background of the minister's wife . . .'

'I knew it! I knew it!' said Edie, her pale eyes shining behind her glasses. 'Scandal!'

'No, nothing like that,' said Hamish sternly, 'and I won't be telling you, Edie, if you keep interrupting.'

'Go on.'

'That play of hers, when she was a lassie, was performed at the university and got rave reviews. She was approached by a major film company. They wanted to buy the rights.'

'Oh, my. What did she do?'

'Her parents were Calvinists and against the movies. They made her turn it down. But I happen to know – if you tell anyone this, I'll kill ye!'

'No, no. Go on. Have a biscuit.'

Hamish selected a foil-wrapped Penguin chocolate biscuit and began to peel off the wrapping with maddening slowness. Then he took a bite and looked at Edie solemnly.

'I happen to know that Eileen Jessop is sending her film off tae Hollywood to some big producer. It's a deadly secret. She hasnae even told her husband.'

He smiled sweetly at Edie's astonished face. He finished his biscuit and drained his cup and stood up.

'But if you get any more attacks from the locals, Edie, you should tell me.'

'Oh, I will, Hamish. And I won't breathe a word.'

Hamish turned in the doorway. 'See that you don't.'

Edie's next visitor was Holly Andrews.

'We put Eileen Jessop in her place,' said Holly. 'It's a bit vain, don't you think, Edie, her wanting us to take time off from our homes to act in her wee bittie film when we could all be stars.'

'We're all thinking this television thing is

going to be shown,' said Edie. 'But there's a jinx on it already. One of the camera crew said they were getting worried on BBC Scotland that it might be tasteless to show it at all in view of the deaths. I think we were all a bit hard on Eileen. Come to think of it, I think my part could do with more work. I'm going up to Eileen's to say I'll be available for more filming.'

Holly was jealous of Eileen's friendship with Ailsa. 'She puts on airs because she's the minister's wife, but I tell you this, Edie, if she shows that tosh she's filmed outside of Drim, we'll be a laughing stock.'

Edie leaned forward, her face intense in the gloom of her living room. 'If I tell you something, Holly, something about Eileen, will you promise not to breathe a word?'

'I'm a clam. You know me. I wouldn't say a word to a soul.'

Holly's eyes grew rounder and rounder as Edie repeated what she had heard from Hamish Macbeth.

'So you're not to say anything, mind!' cautioned Edie as Holly made her way out.


Colin Jessop had gone off to Inverness, and Eileen was alone that evening. She felt depressed and let down.

She walked to the manse window and looked down the drive. And then she saw the village women, done up in their best, walking up the drive, happy and chattering, headed by Edie Aubrey.

She went and opened the door. 'We've just been thinking,' said Edie excitedly, 'that it would do no harm to let you film a bit more.'

'If you really want to,' said Eileen, surprised.

There was a chorus of 'Yes, yes,' as they all crowded into the manse.

Eileen smiled with relief and went to get her camera.

A busy and energetic evening was spent, busy because, not being able to build sets, Eileen had used the interiors of several of the older cottages, so they moved from house to house. Eileen returned to the manse with Ailsa.

'How marvellous they all were,' said Eileen. 'So enthusiastic and everyone acting so well. I could hardly believe it.'

Ailsa grinned. 'You've Hamish Macbeth to thank for that. Man, he must be the best liar in the Highlands, and that's saying something.'

'What do you mean?'

'I didn't let on, Eileen, but Hamish told Edie Aubrey that when your play was put on at the university it got rave reviews and you were approached by a major film company, but that your parents were Calvinists and against the movies and wouldn't let you sign the contract, but now you were going to send this film off to Hollywood.'

'They never believed such a load of rubbish!'

"Course they did. Macbeth told Edie he would kill her if she told anyone.'

'This is awful. We must put them right.'

'Why? You're having fun, aren't you?'

'But you didn't believe it. Why?'

'Because we're friends and you would have told me.'

Eileen grinned. 'I've a bottle of champagne someone gave me two Christmases ago at the bottom of my wardrobe. We'll open it now.'

She longed to tell Ailsa what Sheila had said, but Sheila had told her not to tell anyone. Eileen only hoped Ailsa would not be angry when, if, she ever found out.

Sunday arrived in Lochdubh, wet and misty and warm, 'a great day for the midges', as the locals described the weather.

It was as if the whole Highland world had ground to a halt. It was hard to think that only recently the village had been crowded with pressmen looking for rooms.

Hamish Macbeth, as he went about his domestic chores, thought how easy it would be to let all thoughts of the murder go. Leave it to Lovelace.

And yet, he had not been able to find that tramp Sean Fitz.

Hamish had given up waiting for Sheila to phone and give him some explanation of why she had not turned up at the restaurant.

He decided to drive out and try once more to find Sean. He remembered two years ago, when he was out on his rounds, seeing the shambling figure of the tramp trudging along some road or other.

He began his search again. It was only after a morning of fruitless hunting that he remembered the tramp was religious, a Roman Catholic. He began to check Catholic church after Catholic church, until at Dornoch he found that Sean had been sighted at mass the evening before.

Hamish had some mad hope that if he found the tramp, that if Patricia had been seen somewhere far from the scene of the murder and could therefore be cleared, she would recover her memory.

The frustrating thing was that Sean could be cosily ensconced in some croft somewhere, drinking tea, while he drove past on the road outside. By three in the afternoon, he realized he had not eaten and was hungry.

Finding himself in the main street of Golspie, he went into a café and ordered a sausage roll and beans and a pot of strong tea.

He turned over the suspects in his mind. The more he thought about it, the more he decided that it must surely be a member of the television company. And if it was a member of the television company, it must be someone prone to violence.

He finished his meal and decided to give up the search for Sean and return to the police station and see if he could hack into Blair's reports once more.

But he drove slowly back, still looking to the right and left, hoping to see the tramp.

By the time he reached Lochdubh, the drizzle had thickened to a steady downpour and the waterfront was deserted and glistening in the rain.

He made himself a cup of tea and carried it through to the police office. He played back the answering machine, but there were no messages at all.

He switched on the computer and keyed in Blair's password but this time could not get into the reports. He swore and switched off the machine and stared into space.

There was a knock at the kitchen door, and he went to answer it. Jimmy Anderson stood there. 'Let me in, Hamish. I'm getting fair soaked.'

'The weather had to break sometime.'

'Aye,' said Jimmy, taking off his raincoat and hanging it up on a peg behind the door. 'And folks say, "Can't grumble, we needed the rain," and it always irritates the hell out o' me. It'd take a year o' drought for the Highlands to dry up.'

He sat down at the kitchen table. 'I'm sick o' the Highlands, Hamish. I'm sick o' Lovelace. I never thought I would want Blair back again.

I'm thinking of getting a transfer to Glasgow. See a bit of life. Got that whisky?'

'Yes, and I hope you've some gossip for me.'

'Nothing much. Your friend Patricia still seems to have lost her memory.'

'What about *The Case of the Rising Tides*? Does that still go on?'

'Aye, and it's a pity Patricia couldn't see the changes. That Mary Hoyle is the sort of actress she'd love. No bare tits there.'

Hamish took down the bottle of malt whisky and poured two glasses. Then he lit the wood-burning stove in the kitchen to try to dispel some of the damp.

'I've been thinking,' he said, stretching out his long legs and staring at his large boots, 'that the most likely person with a motive would be one of the television company. You've surely been digging into their backgrounds.'

'Yes, every damn one o' them.'

'What about Harry Frame?'

'The biggest scandal in his background is that he's actually English. Gossip has it that he thought this Scottish independence lark was a good way to get an identity and get backing. He puts it about that he was educated in England but born in Glasgow. Actually he was born to respectable middle-class parents in Somerset. If, say, by some wild flight o' the imagination, Penelope found that out, I hardly think he would kill her.'

'I wish it would turn out to be him,' said

Hamish moodily. 'Here, Jimmy, that's good whisky, not water. You're supposed to sip it.'

'If your whisky dries up, so does my gossip.'

Hamish refilled his glass.

'What about Giles Brown?' he asked.

'The director? Well, there's a thing. You wouldn't think that wee man could say boo to a goose, but he socked a copper.'

'When? Where?'

'It was in Florida a few years ago. He was filming for some television travel show about British tourists abroad. Some American copper tried to move him on, and Giles lost his rag and socked him. Got two nights in the pokey before the lawyers could get him out. But look at the time factor. He was giving the directions. He hardly had time to run off through the mist and tip her over, or, as she said, drag her over.'

'What if Penelope got it wrong?' mused Hamish. 'She was dying when she told me. What if no one pulled her over, but she got one quick push from behind?'

'That would put that delicious wee blonde, Sheila Burford, in the frame.'

'Hardly. She heard her scream and ran towards the sound. What about Fiona King?'

'Done a couple of times for possession of drugs. Had a catfight with the woman she was living with, police called, shouting and screaming, lovers' tiff, nothing much there.'

'What about Penelope's past? Nothing there at all?'

'Nothing more than I've told you.'

Hamish leaned back in his chair and tilted the liquid in his glass. 'You know, the murder of Penelope confuses things. Let's get back to Jamie Gallagher. Angus Harris has a temper, Angus Harris finds his friend was cheated and Angus Harris stood to gain a good bit of money which he must have felt, as the legatee of Stuart's will, he had been done out of. That would have been a good, solid motive. Where was he when Penelope was killed?'

'Touring about, but no alibi. But why would he kill Penelope?'

'Chust supposing,' said Hamish, becoming excited, 'that he killed Jamie Gallagher, but that someone like Fiona, Harry or Giles killed Penelope.'

'Farfetched.'

'So let's take another leap of the imagination. Where was Mary Hoyle on the day of Penelope's murder?'

'Why her? No one checked. Why should they?'

'I haven't seen her in anything for a while,' said Hamish slowly. 'Look at it this way: The original idea of the script was to have sex and a stunner in the main part. What if Mary Hoyle got Harry's ear and pointed out how much better she would be in the part?'

'And he says they've already got someone, so she bumps Penelope off? Come on, Hamish!'

'I haven't met her. Is she at the hotel?'

'Aye, with the others. But you'd better not approach her or you'll have Harry Frame running to Lovelace.'

'There's nothing to stop me having dinner at the hotel this evening.'

'Except your wages.'

'I can afford it once in a blue moon. I'd chust like to meet her.'

'Suit yourself. More whisky?'


That evening, Hamish changed into his one good suit. He would really need to buy a pair of shoes to go with it, he thought as he pulled on his boots. He drove to the hotel and went into the manager, Mr Johnson's, office.

'I would like to meet this Mary Hoyle,' he said.

'You might be in luck. The rest have gone down to the Napoli. She's in the dining room, I think.'

'Any hope of a cheap dinner? Your prices are awfy steep.'

'All right, you moocher, but order the trout and nothing else. We've got more trout than we know what to do with. It's Jenkins's night off. Tell the waitress, Bessie, to give your bill to me.'

Hamish thanked him and went through to the dining room. He recognized Mary Hoyle, sitting at a corner table, reading a manuscript.

229

As he approached, he saw from the title page that the manuscript was the television printed run-off of *The Case of the Rising Tides*.

'Excuse me, Miss Hoyle.' She was an attractive woman with dark hair and a clever face, not beautiful, but with a certain presence. Her eyes were striking, being large and green.

She looked up inquiringly. He sat down opposite her. 'I am Hamish Macbeth, the policeman at Lochdubh. Don't worry. I'm off duty and off the case. I just wanted to tell you how much I admire your acting.'

She smiled. 'That is very kind of you.' Her voice was low and throaty.

The waitress came up. 'I'll have the trout, Bessie,' said Hamish. He looked around. 'But I don't want to be bothering Miss Hoyle ...'

'Oh, stay where you are. I'm nearly finished.'

'And how are you getting on?' asked Hamish.

'Very well. It's an easy part.'

'You must be playing a different character to the one portrayed by Penelope Gates.'

'Yes, I persuaded Harry that he was on the wrong track trying to sex it up. Play it straight and it could run forever. Harry saw sense at last.'

'Did you know him before?'

'Of course. The theatre and television world in Scotland is very small. We all know each other.'

'So you knew Penelope Gates?'

'I met her at a couple of parties. She wasn't an actress. Just a body.'

With a flash of Highland intuition, Hamish said, 'When you heard on the grapevine that Harry was going to do this series, you went after the main part, only to be told he wanted Penelope.'

'Who told you that?'

'Someone or other,' said Hamish vaguely. He longed to ask her where she was on the day of the murder but did not dare go that far for fear she would complain to Harry, who would promptly complain to Lovelace. 'How are you enjoying Patricia's book?' he asked instead.

'It's a bit old-fashioned, even for the sixties. More like a between-the-wars detective story. It doesn't have the pace of a Christie or the brilliance of a Sayers, but it's all right, a bit dull.'

'I've never read it.'

She smiled and handed over the manuscript. 'You can have this. Now if you'll excuse me . . .?'

'Grand talking to you.'

Hamish watched her leave the dining room. Bessie brought his trout, which he picked at while his mind raced. Forget the murder of Jamie. Here was a good motive for the murder of Penelope.

He finished his meal, told Bessie to take his bill to Mr Johnson and went out. Sheila

Burford was just coming into the reception area. She saw him and coloured slightly.

'I'm very sorry I stood you up, Hamish,' she said. 'Something came up.'

But Hamish no longer saw her as an attractive girl but as a possible source of information. 'Come into the bar,' he urged. 'I want a wee word with you.'

'Just a short time, then,' said Sheila reluctantly. Using a funeral as an excuse, she had gone down to Glasgow, where she had registered her own film and television company. Then she'd taken Eileen's cut and edited film with her own name on it as producer to Scottish Television. She was still waiting to hear what they thought of it.

She said she only wanted a glass of tonic water, and Hamish had the same, just in case the dreadful Lovelace came in and caught him drinking whisky.

'So what do you want to talk about?' she asked.

'Mary Hoyle.'

Sheila looked at him in surprise. She had somehow expected Hamish to ask her out again.

'What about her?'

'Did you know she was after the part of Lady Harriet before Penelope got it?'

'No, but I can see why she would expect Harry to give it to her.'

'Her being the better actress?'

'Well, no, because she hadn't had any significant work for some time, and she and Harry used to live together.'

Hamish's eyes gleamed. 'There's a thing. I wonder where she was on the day of Penelope's murder.'

'You mean Mary Hoyle would come all the way up from Glasgow on the off chance of bumping Penelope off, that she would climb up the mountain on a misty day and just happen to pull Penelope over!'

The excitement left Hamish's hazel eyes. 'Now you put it like that, it does sound daft. Still, I'd like to know where she was on the day of the murder.'

'You're a policeman. You ask her.'

'I cannae. That beast Lovelace might get to hear of it, and I'm off the case. You couldnae ask her yourself?'

'Just like that!'

'You could chust sort of sneak it into the conversation. I know, you thought you saw her in Drim on that day. Please.'

'I'll try,' said Sheila doubtfully.

'And you'll phone me?'

'Oh, all right.'

'You won't forget?'

'Okay, okay, I'll ask her. Now can I go to bed?'

Hamish stood up. 'I'll wait to hear from you tomorrow. Don't let me down.'

\* \* \*

When Hamish got back to the police station, he felt restless. He decided to take *The Case of the Rising Tides* to bed.

It was certainly soporific reading. But he managed to get halfway through it before he finally fell asleep, the papers scattered around the bed.

Sheila almost forgot Hamish's request, but the following day during a break in the filming, Harry instructed her to take a cup of coffee to Mary's caravan.

She almost felt like refusing and saying she was not a waitress, when she saw a way of asking that question for Hamish.

Mary Hoyle was creaming her face when Sheila knocked and entered the caravan. 'Good, put it down there,' said Mary without turning around.

'Something's been puzzling me,' said Sheila.

'What?' said Mary absently.

'I think I saw you in Drim on the day of Penelope's murder.'

Mary threw a soiled tissue into the wastepaper basket and turned round. 'What's your name?'

'Sheila Burford.'

'I wish Harry would employ sensible, intelligent girls instead of little tarts who are all bust and no brains. You are mistaken. I was not in Drim on the day of the murder.'

'Where were you?'

'Do you know who you are speaking to? Get out of here and find something to do. That is, unless you are expected to do anything other than allow Harry and the other men to gawp down your cleavage.'

Sheila, who was wearing a low-necked blouse, turned and left the caravan. Damn them all. If only she could sell that film of Eileen's.

She took out her mobile phone and called Hamish Macbeth.

'Thanks, Sheila,' said Hamish when she reported the conversation.

Sheila remembered how nice Hamish was compared to the people she was working with. 'I'm really sorry I stood you up, Hamish. I tell you what, I'll take you for dinner on Wednesday evening at the Napoli. It's a firm date.'

'Grand,' said Hamish. 'I'll be there.'

He rang off and stared into space while his mind raced. If only he could get down to Glasgow and start ferreting into Mary Hoyle's movements on the day of the murder. Perhaps he could phone in sick. Perhaps –

There was a knock at the door.

Hamish opened it.

The sun was shining once more. A tramp squinted up at him. 'Any chance of a cup of tea?'

Hamish beamed.

'Come in, Sean Fitz,' he said. 'You're chust the man I want to see.'

# Chapter Nine

*Did ye not hear it? – No; 'twas but the wind,*
*Or the car rattling o'er the stony street.*
                                        – Lord Byron

'This is verra good of you, Officer,' said Sean, eating biscuits and drinking tea.

He was an old bearded man with young-looking, light grey eyes in a tanned and wrinkled face. His clothes smelled of peat smoke and heather, but nothing more sinister. Sean was a clean tramp.

'As a matter of fact, I've been looking for you,' said Hamish.

'It wisnae me that took Mrs Hegarty's knickers off the washing line, whateffer she might say,' said the tramp, looking frightened.

'Relax, Sean,' said Hamish, 'Nothing criminal. Now, have you heard about the murders?'

'Over at Drim. Aye.'

'There's one thing I want to know. There's a writer called Patricia Martyn-Broyd. You probably don't know her . . .'

'I know everyone,' said the tramp. His eyes ranged round the kitchen. 'I'm still a wee bit hungry.'

Hamish went to the freezer and took out a plastic bag of stew. 'I'll heat this up for you.'

'Verra kind, I'm sure.'

'Now, Sean, while the stew's heating up, tell me how you know Patricia, the writer woman.'

'I called at her cottage . . . oh, maybe a few months back.'

'I didnae know you had been up here that long. Where were you before that?'

'Down south, but it iss not the same as the Highlands.'

'So tell me what happened when you called at the cottage.'

'I asked her for a cup of tea and a bite and said I could do some odd jobs for her in return. Herself looked down her nose and said, "Be off with you or I'll call the police."'

'So you know what she looks like,' said Hamish eagerly. 'This is what I want to know. On the day of the murder of that actress, Patricia said she was in a state and chust driving about. She has a white Metro. Did you see her anywhere?'

'White Metro, no. That stew smells rare, Hamish.'

'Bide your time, Sean. It won't even be thawed out yet. What do you mean, "white Metro, no"?'

'Chust that. I couldnae be sure, mind. I wass between here and Drim and . . . Here, you're not trying to pin the murder on me!'

'No, no, Sean,' said Hamish soothingly. 'What did you see?'

'It wass misty, all swirling about, coming and going. The car wass going that slowly, I had to step out o' the road. Herself had the dark glasses on and I 'member thinking, how could she see on a misty day in those things, and she had a headscarf on, dark blue.'

'So how could you tell it was her?'

'I thought when I first saw her she looked like a witch. It wass herself all right.'

'But the car. She wasn't driving a white Metro?'

'I'm no good at cars, Hamish. It wass small and black.'

'But you are really sure it was her?'

'Aye.'

'And it was between here and Drim. What time of day?'

'I'd been sleeping in the heather and had not long got up. It must haff been about six in the morning.'

Hamish stared at him for a long moment. 'Wait here, Sean,' he said. 'I've got something to do.'

He went through to the bedroom and picked up the spilled pages of manuscript and began searching through them feverishly until he had found what he wanted. Then he went through to the police office and phoned Jimmy Anderson.

'I think I might be on to something, Jimmy,' he said.

'Hurry up, man. Thon Martyn-Broyd woman's got her memory back and is about to be discharged and we're all going up there with Lovelace to grovel and apologize.'

'Is there a car firm in Strathbane where you can rent a car, a place that would be open all night?'

'In Strathbane? Man, everything closes down as tight as a drum at six o'clock in the evening.'

'Thanks.'

'What's it about?'

'Phone me later and I'll let you know.'

Hamish had to fret and wait until he had fed the tramp and given him a few pounds. Then he took a statement from him and told him there would be more food and money for him if he reported to the police station the following day.

Then he set out for Cnothan.

Sheila Burford's mobile phone rang. The actors stopped acting, the camera stopped rolling and Harry Frame shouted, 'I told everyone to switch their phones off.'

'I'm sorry,' said Sheila, taking the ringing mobile phone out of her bag. 'I'm expecting an important call.'

'You're fired,' shouted Harry, but Sheila was already walking away, the phone to her ear.

Fiona King, watching Sheila, saw the sudden look of radiant joy on the girl's face as she tucked the phone back into her bag.

Sheila hurried away from the filming and towards the manse.

The minister answered the door and reluctantly let her in, damning her as another of those friends who had so altered his hitherto submissive wife's personality for the worse.

'What is it, Sheila?' asked Eileen, who was rolling pastry in the kitchen.

The minister went into his study and slammed the door. 'Come outside a moment,' whispered Sheila. 'Great news.'

Eileen went out to the garden with her.

Sheila swung round to face her. 'We're a success! Scottish Television want us both in Glasgow as soon as possible. They're buying your film!'

'Oh, my,' said Eileen, dazed. 'Do I have to tell Colin? He'll start ranting and raging again. I thought I had something on him, I thought he was having an affair with a woman down in Inverness, but he says he was comforting a poor widow, and it's all in my dirty mind, and he's suddenly stopped going away on trips.'

'Is he out today?'

'Yes, he's got to go to Lochdubh to see Mr Wellington, the minister over there, about something.'

'What time?'

'About two o'clock.'

'I've got to pack up, and so have you. I'll call round for you. You can leave him a note.'

'I'll do it,' said Eileen. 'I was going to leave him anyway.'

Ailsa Kennedy came up the garden towards them. 'Not a word,' hissed Sheila. 'I don't want anyone to know until the contract's signed.'

Sheila ran off. 'What was all that about?' asked Ailsa.

'Oh, nothing much,' said Eileen, feeling disloyal, but desperately improvising. 'She just wanted to know if I would be in a crowd scene.'

'And what did you say?'

'I said Colin wouldn't approve.'

Ailsa snorted. 'He can't say anything about anything after the way he's been going on.'

'That's just the trouble. He says nothing has been going on and I have no proof.'

'That's daft. Ignore him. Come and join us. We're all on in a few moments.'

'No ... I'll stay here.' Eileen held up her floury hands. 'I'm baking.'

'Your husband's got you in a right state. I've a good mind to go in there and give him a piece of my mind, minister or no minister.'

'I'll see you later, Ailsa. I promise. I've got to get on.'

Eileen served her husband lunch and then waited impatiently until at last he got in the car and drove off. She hurried to her bedroom – she and Colin had had separate bedrooms for some years now – and began to feverishly pack up her belongings.

When she heard a car drive up, she nearly fainted with fright, but soon she heard Sheila's voice calling her.

She lugged two heavy suitcases down the stairs. The manse door had been open, and Sheila was standing in the hall.

'I'd better leave a note for him,' said Eileen. She left the cases and went into Colin's clinically neat study.

She seized a piece of paper and wrote, 'I'm fed up with you. I want a divorce. I've left you. Eileen.'

Then she slammed the study door behind her and went out to where Sheila was loading her suitcases into the boot of the car.

'Off we go,' said Sheila as the minister's wife climbed in beside her. 'Goodbye, Drim!'

'Goodbye,' echoed Eileen with a happy smile. She thought briefly of her husband and then shrugged. She felt she had finally become unchained from a maniac.


'I hate this place. God, how I hate this place,' muttered Hamish Macbeth as he started his investigations again in and around Cnothan.

The standard and cold reply to his questions was, 'We aye mind our own business around here, Macbeth' – from a village, reflected Hamish, as notorious as Salem during the witch-hunts for minding everyone else's business but their own.

By the time he stopped in at the Tudor Restaurant – fake beams, fake horse brasses, dried flowers, and what was a restaurant called Tudor doing in the Highlands? – he was feeling as sour as the residents. As the waitress slammed down a plate of 'Henry the Eighth Chicken Salad – throw the bones over your shoulder to the dogs!' in front of him, he had more or less decided to give the whole thing up.

He ate his cold dry chicken flanked by limp lettuce and wished he were Henry VIII and could have whoever in the back prepared this muck put in the stocks. He finished his dreadful meal with a cup of coffee of a brand publicized by a well-known British transvestite, and the coffee was as much coffee as the publicist was a woman. He fished in his pocket for his wallet to pull out a note, and as he did so a piece of paper fluttered to the floor. He picked it up. Priscilla Halburton-Smythe's London number.

He paid for his meal and went to the nearest phone box. The graffiti inside reflected the bitterness of the inhabitants. As he dialled Priscilla's number, he saw that someone had scrawled across the board holding the phone instructions 'She doesn't love you. Go fuck yourself.' Malice, thought Hamish, inserting a phone card and dialling the number, gives the graffiti writer a certain vicious insight into what might hurt most.

He had become so used to rejection that day that he was almost amazed when Priscilla answered the phone after the first ring.

After the preliminary pleasantries, Hamish explained why he was in Cnothan.

'Doesn't this woman have any friends?' asked Priscilla.

'Not a one.'

'Does she go to church?'

'Yes.'

'Then if she wanted to ask a favour like borrowing a car, she might go to the manse. Have you asked there?'

'No, I didnae even think of it.'

'You're slipping,' said Priscilla cheerfully.

'This damn place is enough to make any-one's brain slip a few cogs. Are you coming up here soon?'

'In about two weeks' time.'

Hamish said goodbye and rang off. Two weeks! She would be home again in only two weeks. He felt so excited that he had to calm down by forcibly reminding himself that he did not love her any more.

At the manse he was greeted by the min-ister's wife, Mrs Struthers. 'What is it, Officer?' she demanded sharply. 'I am busy.'

He masked his irritation and said, 'Did Miss Martyn-Broyd at any time ask you for the loan of a car?'

'We don't lend anyone our car,' she said sharply. 'Our insurance doesn't cover anyone else driving it.'

He thanked her and touched his cap and was turning away when he swung back. 'But did she ask you?'

'Well, yes, and so late at night, too. I told her she could not have it.'

'Did you suggest anyone who might lend her one?'

'I said she could try old Mr Ludlow.'

'And where does Mr Ludlow live?'

'He is not very well, and I would not like to think of him being troubled.'

'I am a police officer, and you are obstructing me in my enquiries. Ludlow's address, please!'

'Mr Ludlow to you, Officer. Oh, very well. He lives at Five, The Glebe, down at the loch.'

Hamish walked down to where the grey waters of the loch lay sullen under a low grey sky. The great ugly dam soared above the loch. He stopped and stared at it, imagining it cracking, then bursting, then the deluge crashing through to drown the whole of Cnothan and everyone in it.

He found Mr Ludlow's cottage. There was a garage next to the cottage.

He knocked at the door and waited.

There was a shuffling sound inside, like that of some hibernating animal turning in its sleep. The shuffling noises grew nearer, and the door was opened a crack and a rheumy eye stared at Hamish.

'Mr Ludlow?'

'I havenae done anything. Go away.'

'Nobody said you had,' said Hamish patiently. 'I just want a wee word with you.'

The door opened wider. Mr Ludlow was an old man on whose face a lifetime of bitterness and discontent was mapped out in the deep, dismal wrinkles on a face as grey as elephant's skin.

'Did you lend your car at any time to Patricia Martyn-Broyd?'

There was a long silence. An omen of crows suddenly tumbled overhead, cawing and cackling, and then they were gone.

'Aye, and if I did?'

'May I see your car?'

The old man grumbled out in a pair of battered carpet slippers. He led the way to the garage, took out a key and opened the padlock which secured the door. Inside was an old black Ford.

'When did she ask you for a loan of it?'

'It wass the night afore that tarty bit was murdered, her what bares her body. Miss Martyn-Broyd, I knew her from the church, she says her car had broken down. She had got me out o' bed to answer the door. I didn't want to let her have it.'

'But she took out a handful of notes, so you let her have it,' guessed Hamish.

'Aye, well, I'm a pensioner, and money's tight.'

'Chust about as tight as that hole in your arse that you talk through,' said Hamish.

There was a stunned silence, neither of them able to believe what they had just heard.

'What did you say?' demanded Mr Ludlow at last.

'I said, chust about as tight as that hole in the road over at Crask,' said Hamish, improvising wildly. 'I'll be on my way, Mr Ludlow.'

'I didnae do anything wrong?' he asked.

'No, nothing,' said Hamish, and added maliciously, 'provided your insurance covers another driver.'

He had the satisfaction of seeing from the sudden fright in Mr Ludlow's eyes that it probably did not.

As he walked back to his police Land Rover, he had a new respect for Sergeant MacGregor. If I lived here, thought Hamish, I would end up stark, staring mad.

He opened the Land Rover door. Then he stopped, one foot raised, his mouth a little open. Those two threads of blue tweed he had found on the mountain, the day Jamie died. Could they have been from something Patricia had been wearing?

He got in and drove to her cottage. She had been released from hospital but was obviously not home yet.

He stared at the cottage in frustration. Then he felt in the guttering above the door where locals usually hid a door key, but there was nothing there. Perhaps Patricia had not even bothered to lock up. He tried the door handle, and to his relief the door opened.

He went in and searched for the bedroom, finding it off the kitchen at the back.

There was a wardrobe over on the far wall. He swung open the door. There were a few tailored suits and dresses and, on a shelf above, an assortment of hats.

He slowly lifted out a blue tweed suit and laid it on the bed and began to go over it inch by inch. And then down at the hem of the skirt, he found where two threads had been tugged out.

He sat down suddenly on the bed. He could hardly go back to Lochdubh and find these threads and present them as evidence, for he would be charged with suppressing evidence.

He was sure now she had murdered both Jamie and Penelope.

And then he heard cars driving up outside. He went to the window. In the first black official car was Patricia with Superintendent Peter Daviot; in the second were Lovelace, Macnab and Anderson.

He went to the outside door and opened it. Peter Daviot was helping Patricia from the car. Lovelace and the two detectives had gathered around.

'We must assure you again, Miss Martyn-Broyd, of our deepest apologies,' Mr Daviot was saying, when Lovelace suddenly saw Hamish standing there

'What are you doing?' he shouted.

They all turned to stare at him.

'I think we had better all go inside,' said Hamish.

'You'd better have a damned good reason to explain what you are doing in Miss Martyn-Broyd's cottage,' said Lovelace.

But Patricia, with an odd little smile on her face, had already walked forward. Hamish stood aside, and they all trooped into the parlour.

Hamish was suddenly terrified. All Patricia had to do was deny his accusations. He had no real proof. She could admit to borrowing Ludlow's car but say that she'd had to get away, that in her distress she had forgotten to explain she was not in her own car. But he had gone this far, so he had to take it to the end.

'Perhaps if we all sit down,' said Hamish, 'I'll explain what I am doing here.'

'Tea?' said Patricia, smiling all around.

'Not now,' said Hamish. 'I haff a story for you, Miss Martyn-Broyd, that is stranger than any fiction. Josh Gates did not kill Jamie

Gallagher. You did. I think you waited until you saw them all leave. You had not thought of murder then. You noticed that Jamie had not come down. You were probably hidden somewhere beside the path. You went on up. You saw Jamie sitting there, and the impulse took you. You picked up a rock and brained him with it, and then just went away. You felt that the man who had sneered at your work, who had debased it, was finally dead and gone.

'But then there was Penelope Gates. She, too, sneered at you and told you how you had been tricked. You had killed once, and you could kill again. Somehow you knew from the script that she would be up on the mountain. In your book *The Case of the Rising Tides*, the murderer borrows a car so that his own car will not be recognized, so you borrowed a black Ford from Mr Ludlow in Cnothan, calling on him late at night and paying him a lot to lend you that car.

'At around six in the morning on the day of the murder you were spotted by the tramp Sean Fitz, heading for Drim. I think you found by accident that other path up the mountain. You would want to avoid the main path, too many people coming and going.

'Sound carries verra clearly up there. You heard the instruction to Penelope to stand on that outcrop of rock. You were hidden underneath. When you knew she was in position, you stood up and grasped her ankle and

251

jerked her over your head, and she went flying down the mountain. You escaped in the thick mist, got in the car, drove around and finally went to the Sutherland Arms Hotel for lunch. Then you returned the car to Ludlow.'

Lovelace opened his mouth to say something, but Daviot held up a warning finger. All looked at Patricia.

'What a load of rubbish,' she fluted. 'Yes, I did borrow a car, but I was so dazed and unhappy, I did not know what I was doing that day. Yes, I may have gone near Drim, but I did not go up on that mountain.' She spread her hands in an appealing gesture and looked at Lovelace. 'Have I not endured enough?'

She might get away with it, thought Hamish, and even if it cost him his job, she would not get away with it. He would need to confess about those two threads of cloth.

He said instead, 'You were seen going up the mountain on the day Jamie Gallagher was murdered. I chust found that out today. A crofter saw you and didn't think anything of it at the time, thinking you were part of the TV crew.'

'You're lying,' said Patricia flatly.

Too right, thought Hamish dismally. But he looked straight at her and said evenly, 'I am only glad you will not profit from your crimes because after you are charged with these murders, the sales of your books will be immense, and all over the world, too. You will be a truly famous writer, and that is a distinction you do not deserve.'

Patricia stared at him.

Lovelace stood up. 'This is enough,' he said. 'I have heard about you, Macbeth, and your behaviour has been disgraceful. Breaking into this poor woman's cottage –'

'I did it,' said Patricia.

Everyone froze except Hamish, who felt himself go almost limp with relief.

She gave a shrug and said in an almost merry voice, 'It was justice, don't you see? They were killing Lady Harriet, so they both had to go. I do not regret it. You are right. I did not mean to kill that Gallagher man. But I did not lurk around waiting until they all had left. I was late. I thought they were all still up there and that perhaps I could get them to change their minds. But there was no one there. I wandered about. And then I saw Jamie, sitting on the edge of the heather in front of the scree. After that I do not know what happened until he was dead at my feet and I was standing with a bloody rock in my hand. I hurled it away as hard as I could. I do not regret it.

'Penelope Gates was everything I hated, crude and vulgar and vicious. She had to go. I do not regret her death, either.'

'But two murders!' exclaimed Daviot.

'But they were guilty of infanticide,' said Patricia with a sort of dreadful patience.

'They killed my child. They were killing Lady Harriet.'

Lovelace charged her with the murders. She kept looking at Hamish. When Lovelace had finished, she said, 'Hamish, will I be really famous?'

'Yes,' he said sadly. 'Very famous indeed.'

'Then that's all right,' she said briskly, getting to her feet. 'Shall we go?'

'Wait a minute,' said Hamish as she was being led out. 'Patricia, why did you ask for my help to clear your name?'

'Oh, I thought you were the only person I had to fear,' said Patricia with a little smile. 'These other gentlemen are so stupid. It worked for a bit, didn't it?'

'Yes, it worked,' said Hamish. 'And did you really lose your memory?'

'No, I did not. I simply became weary of the act and decided to find it again. I wrote about an amnesia case in one of my books and had read a great deal on the subject, enough to trick the psychiatrist. How did you guess it was me?'

One more lie wouldn't matter, thought Hamish. He hoped they would forget about that crofter he said had seen Patricia on the mountain.

'It was Detective Jimmy Anderson who suggested that you might have used another car.'

'How odd,' said Patricia. 'I would have thought him as stupid as the rest.'

She was led out.

Daviot remained behind with Hamish. 'Good work,' he said. 'This lets Blair off the hook, and I'm glad of it. He's a good man and probably thought she had done it all along.'

Hamish groaned inwardly, but better Blair than Lovelace.

'I shall be glad to return Lovelace to Inverness,' went on Daviot. 'He ruffled too many feathers at Strathbane, ordering policewomen to do his shopping for him. Not on, in these liberated days.'

'I had best go and get an official statement from that man who lent her the car,' said Hamish.

'Yes,' said Daviot absently. 'This is all going to make us look a bunch of fools with the press.'

'In what way, sir?'

'Well, saying Josh Gates murdered Jamie Gallagher. Bad press, that.'

'But the murders are solved, and you've got them off your back.'

'True. You should consider a move to Strathbane, Hamish.' Hamish, not Macbeth. He was definitely in favour.

'No, sir. I am quite happy where I am. It was Jimmy Anderson who put me on to it.'

'Then why did he not do it himself?'

'He might be frightened he would get into trouble with Lovelace. If you will forgive me for speaking freely, Sir, that man does not like initiative.'

'It will be good to have Blair back.'

A man who disliked initiative just as much as Lovelace, thought Hamish.

'We should not be sitting here,' said Daviot. 'I'd best get the forensic team over here.'

'Why don't you go ahead, sir,' said Hamish. 'The door was open, but I see there's a key on the counter there. I'll lock up and wait outside for the forensic team.'

'Very well.'

Hamish followed him out and stood waiting until Daviot's car had roared off into the distance. Then he went into the bedroom and carefully took the tweed suit off the bed and hung it back in the wardrobe.

Then he sat down to wait for the forensic team. He had plenty of time to reflect on his own stupidity. Patricia had initially got away with both murders through sheer luck. Different car or not, Ludlow could have come forward and told the police. But Hamish had not suspected her, something in Patricia's loneliness of spirit striking a chord in his own. And he had been flattered when she had asked him to help her. She must have been very confident that, owing to the mist and the different car, no one would recognize her. But thanks to her rudeness to one tramp, which had made him remember her vividly, she had been recognized.

He stretched and yawned. Sergeant Mac-Gregor was welcome to Cnothan. What a dump!

The forensic team arrived, and Hamish thankfully left. He went in to Cnothan and took a statement from Mr Ludlow and then made his escape. As he drove down into Lochdubh, a shaft of sunlight was breaking through the grey clouds. Priscilla was coming home. The world was righting itself.

At the police station, he typed up his reports, took off his uniform and put on casual clothes and went out for a stroll.

Mrs Wellington, the minister's wife, bore down on him like a tweedy galleon under full sail. 'Shocking news,' she boomed.

'Yes, I wouldnae have believed a lady like Miss Martyn-Broyd could have committed two murders,' said Hamish.

She looked at him in amazement. 'What are you talking about?'

'Miss Martyn-Broyd has confessed to the murders of Jamie Gallagher and Penelope Gates.'

'Impossible!'

'I am afraid it's true. What are you talking about?'

'Oh, that.' The minister's wife pulled herself together with an effort. 'We have just heard from poor Mr Jessop over at Drim. He's in such a taking. His wife has left him! He phoned to say she had left while he was actually over here visiting us.'

'Neffer!'

'Yes, just gone and taken all her stuff. They were such a devoted couple.'

'I got the impression he bullied that poor woman.'

'Nonsense. I tell you what he thinks happened. It's this television business. It's driven all the women in Drim mad. They all think they were meant to be film stars. Mr Jessop sees nothing but ruin for his poor wife. He says she'll end up on the streets.'

'Oh, I shouldn't think so. She wouldn't make any money.'

'And that's just the sort of nasty callous thing I would expect from you. You haven't been to church in ages. That's what's up with you, Hamish Macbeth.'

'Maybe next Sunday,' said Hamish, sliding around her bulk.

He thought of treating himself to dinner at the Napoli, then remembered that he had a date there with Sheila for the following evening. He bought himself some cold ham from Patel's and went back to his garden and pulled and cleaned a lettuce to make a salad to go with it.

He had an interrupted meal. The news of Patricia's arrest had spread like wildfire, and locals kept coming to the kitchen door to ask for details. At last he settled down in front of the television. There was a good play on BBC 1, so when he heard someone rapping at the kitchen door again, he debated whether to pretend he wasn't at home. But the knocking grew more insistent. With a sigh he got up and opened the door.

Jimmy Anderson stood there. 'Gimme a whisky, for God's sake, man. She isnae fit tae stand trial.'

'Patricia? She's acting again.' Hamish led him in and took the bottle of whisky out of the kitchen cupboard.

'If she's acting, it's too good for anyone to break.'

They went into the living room. Hamish lit the fire. 'The nights are drawing in at last,' he said.

'I came anyway to thank you for giving me the credit,' said Jimmy. 'What put you on to her?'

'She did,' said Hamish. 'Would you believe it? She wanted me to clear her name and so I spent my spare time trying to find out where she was when Penelope was being murdered. And she was so confident I wouldn't find out. I'm just glad it's over. Blair'll be happy.'

'Aye, he's poncing about saying as how he was victimized by a madwoman and that he knew she did it all along. He seems to forget he was the one who insisted Josh Gates murdered Jamie Gallagher.'

'He aye had a convenient memory.'

'Daviot said he thought you'd cracked Patricia by suggesting she would be world famous.'

'It was a gamble, but it paid off. I'd nearly forgotten about her monumental vanity.'

'So we settle back down to a peaceful life, you with your sheep and hens and me with the muggings and stabbings in Strathbane.' He raised his glass. 'Here's tae murder.'

'No, no, man, here's to peace and quiet.'

'Peace and quiet,' said Jimmy solemnly.

They both drank in silence, and then Hamish asked, 'Do you think they'll go ahead with filming the series after all this? There's the relatives of the dead to remember.'

'I think after a certain time has elapsed, they'll run it. They've surely sunk too much money in it already to abandon the whole thing.'

'I suppose so.'

'My lady friend wants to be a writer,' said Jimmy. 'I told her to forget it. They're all mad, that's what I said. Got a girl, Hamish?'

'Maybe,' said Hamish, thinking of Sheila. 'Maybe I have.'

Down in her flat in Glasgow, Sheila and Eileen stared in amazement at the late night news on television. 'It was that writer after all,' said Sheila.

'Hamish must be glad it's all over,' said Eileen.

'Oh, the policeman? I think I was supposed to phone him or something, but with all this

260

success about your film, I forget what it was. Oh, there's something I forgot to tell you. Scottish Television wants to find out when they plan to screen the first episode of *The Case of the Rising Tides* and run your play against it, same evening, same time.'

'But will that work?' asked Eileen. 'I mean, there'll be such a lot of interest in Harry's thing, with the murders. No one will watch my play.'

'They thought of that. They're going to screen it in advance and get all the publicity they hope it will get and then run it again on the Sunday. We're going to be big, Eileen. Right to the top!'


On Wednesday evening, Hamish Macbeth sat in the Napoli and waited for Sheila – and waited. At first he had this really splendid dream, that Priscilla Halburton-Smythe would return to Lochdubh to find him with a brand-new, pretty girlfriend, but as the evening dragged past and she did not come, the dream faded and died.

# Epilogue

*It doesn't much signify whom one marries, for one is sure to find next morning that it was someone else.*

— Samuel Rogers

Now that the murders had been solved and he had made all his statements, Hamish Macbeth moved back into his usual undemanding routine. In anticipation of Priscilla's arrival, he had bought a new pair of shoes to go with his suit, although he convinced himself that he had only bought them because he urgently needed them.

On the day she was due to arrive home, he was suddenly summoned to Strathbane. It transpired that Patricia Martyn-Broyd was evidently genuinely mad as a hatter, but Daviot had suggested that Hamish should try to speak to her, try to see if she were really insane or faking it, as she had so cleverly faked amnesia.

He drove down to Strathbane and to the secure unit of a psychiatric hospital. It was an old Victorian building, sinister in the mist which had rolled in from the oily, polluted sea around Strathbane.

'What's she like?' he asked the grim-faced woman with keys jangling at her waist who conducted him along the long corridors. 'In a straitjacket?'

'No, herself is quiet. No trouble at all.'

She unlocked a door. Hamish walked in and the door was locked behind him.

Patricia was sitting on the floor, rocking back and forth and crooning to herself.

Hamish sat down on the floor beside her. 'Patricia,' he said gently, 'do you know me?'

She stopped rocking and her eyes stared at him and then she started rocking again.

'Are you pretending to be mad, Patricia? It won't do if you are. You don't want to stay in a place like this for the rest o' your life. If you stood trial and went to prison, they would let you have something to write on. You'd be able to sell new books.'

The rocking continued.

'It wass a bad thing you did, Patricia, taking two lives. But if you are acting, you are going to haff to go on like this till the end.'

But she rocked and crooned, seemingly oblivious to his presence.

He gave a little sigh. 'I would ha' thought a lady like yourself would have had more courage. In prison, they have a library and you'd be able to see your books, maybe give talks to the other prisoners.'

No response.

His voice grew harder. 'Did you know what Jamie Gallagher looked like when I found him? The crows had pecked his eyes out. Did you know that Penelope had maybe had a pretty harsh upbringing? And there she lay, crushed and dying of pain on the side o' the mountain. Do you know the horror you caused?'

But she rocked and rocked.

He gave up. He got to his feet. The woman looked through a small square of glass window and promptly unlocked and opened the door.

Hamish walked out and the door was locked behind him.

He went along the corridor. Suddenly he said, 'Excuse me a minute.' He darted silently back along the corridor and looked through the window into Patricia's room.

She was standing by the window with her hands on her hips, looking out. He signalled to the woman urgently to open the door. She came running up and unlocked it.

But when he rushed in, Patricia was once more on the floor, rocking and moaning and crooning.

Hamish stood over her. 'It iss my belief you're a fake. But if you want to stay here with the insane, that's your lookout.'

He waited, but she did not cease her rocking.

He gave an exclamation of disgust and walked out. What should he do? he wondered as he drove to police headquarters. He thought of her stance at the window. Even though her back had been turned to him, it had somehow been the posture of a normal woman.

At police headquarters, he had to wait. Jimmy Anderson told him that Daviot wanted to see him. He waited patiently outside Daviot's room under the grim eye of the secretary, who detested him.

At last he was ushered in. 'This is the psychiatrist, Dr Lodge,' said Daviot. 'He has been working with our prisoner.'

Hamish said that he had a shrewd idea that Patricia was acting. 'That is not the view of Dr Lodge here,' said Daviot.

Hamish had to listen then to a long lecture from Dr Lodge on Patricia's condition. It became clear to Hamish that the psychiatrist had made up his mind that Patricia was mad and he was angry that a village policeman should have been produced to argue with his expert diagnosis.

'It is just that Macbeth here knew the woman,' said Daviot placatingly.

'You are probably not interested in my opinion, Dr Lodge,' said Hamish. 'I not only think her sane, I think she will take her own life. At first she did not mind, thinking only of the publicity the trial would bring her books. But she obviously does not want to stand trial now and go to prison, nor will she want to remain in a psychiatric unit for the rest of her life.'

Another long and tedious lecture, which all boiled down to the fact that Dr Lodge considered it impossible that Patricia would commit suicide. Daviot was obviously impressed as some Scots are by esoteric lectures of which they do not understand one word.

'Thank you, nonetheless, for your input,' said Daviot finally. 'You may go.'

Hamish went into the detectives' room. Blair was back at his desk. 'Here he comes,' said Blair. 'The village idiot. Didn't I say that wumman had done it? If they hadnae taken me off the case, I'd have had it wrapped up.'

'Chust as you had the murder of Jamie Gallagher wrapped up?' asked Hamish.

'Get oot o' here!' roared Blair.

Hamish grinned and walked off. Blair was back and things were back to normal.


As he drove back to Lochdubh, he thought of seeing Priscilla Halburton-Smythe again with a rising feeling of excitement. Once at the police station, he changed into his new suit and good shoes. He drove up to the Tommel Castle Hotel and went into reception. Mr Johnson stopped when he saw him. 'Looking very chic, Hamish. What's the occasion?'

'No occasion,' said Hamish, colouring. 'Priscilla arrived?'

'Oh, didn't you know? She phoned to say she had been delayed in London and doesn't know when she'll get up.'

'Aye, well, thanks for telling me.'

'Did you come hoping to see her?'

'No,' lied Hamish, and improvising wildly. 'Is Fiona King around?'

Mr Johnson looked past him through the open door to the car park. 'I think that's her just arriving.'

Hamish went out to meet Fiona. 'Everything going all right?' he asked.

'Right as rain,' said Fiona.

'Is Sheila around?'

'She got fired and took off ages ago. Don't know where she is. Glasgow, I suppose.'

'Something's been puzzling me,' said Hamish. 'Did you ever go to Angus Macdonald?'

'The seer? Well, yes, I did. A lot of us went over to have our fortunes told.'

She must have said something nasty about Penelope to give the seer the idea that she had killed her, thought Hamish.

He got into the police Land Rover and drove into Lochdubh. Then he thought, surely Priscilla would have phoned, left a message for him.

He ran into the police office and played his answering machine. Nothing, nothing at all. Sheila had gone off without saying goodbye, Priscilla could not come home and yet had not considered him worth even a message.

His gloomy thoughts turned back to the case. He supposed he would always regard it as one of his failures, for surely the evidence that Patricia had committed the murder lay right there in her character. He discounted the fact that Blair had said he knew it was her all along, for Blair crashed through every case, accusing everyone. Misery loves company. He would go over to Drim and see the minister, Colin Jessop.

The minister led him into his study. 'What brings you, Macbeth?'

'I wondered if you had any news from your wife. I wondered if you had heard from her or wanted her traced.'

'I have not heard from her, nor do I want her traced.'

'Why did she take off?'

'It was this TV business. It turned her into a silly woman.'

'Perhaps when she's had a bit of time away, she'll come back home,' said Hamish soothingly.

'In that case,' said the minister waspishly, 'she'll have the door slammed in her face.'

The study door opened and a hard-faced middle-aged blonde woman came in, carrying a tray. 'Time for your tea, dear,' she cooed.

'If that's all, Constable,' said the minister impatiently.

Hamish left, pushing back his cap and scratching his fiery red hair in bewilderment.

What a nasty wee man that minister was, yet it had taken him no time at all to find a replacement for his wife. What was up with one Hamish Macbeth? No one wanted *him*.

He went down to the general stores to buy some groceries. Ailsa Kennedy was behind the counter.

'It is yourself, Hamish,' she said.

'I see the minister's got a new woman,' said Hamish, leaning on the counter.

'Calls her his housekeeper,' said Ailsa.

'Have you heard from Eileen Jessop?'

Ailsa's face darkened. 'No, she just took off without a word to anyone. I thought she was my friend. All the village women believed thon lie you told Edie about Eileen sending her film to Hollywood. Of course, they know it's a lot of rubbish now. They're not wanted for any more crowd scenes, so they're all a bit flat.'

'Well, it'll stop them throwing bricks at each other,' said Hamish heartlessly.

But as he paid for his groceries and made his way home, he had to confess to feeling pretty flat himself.


Eileen's play had been kept a secret, and the women of Drim did not know about it until Holly Andrews ran around the village waving a newspaper. The advance reviews for *The Witch of Drim* were enthusiastic.

'And she never even said a word to you,'

Holly Andrews told Ailsa. 'Well, I always said she was sly.'

On the night of the first performance, the whole of Drim crowded round their television sets. Ailsa had invited Holly Andrews, Edie and Alice to watch it with her. At first they cheered and laughed and hugged each other as they watched the show. But when it was over and Ailsa said, 'Eileen really is brilliant,' Holly said, 'Aye, and she'll get a lot of money, and here's us, who slaved our guts out for her, not even being invited to the press conference or getting a bit of money.'

'That's right,' said Edie, goggling at her. 'She'd better not show herself here again.'


Eileen's play was shown on television in Scotland and then on national on the following Sunday, where it successfully took away a large chunk of the audience for *The Case of the Rising Tides*.

Harry's TV detective series got panned by the critics and suffered badly in comparison with Eileen's play.

'Do you know,' said Eileen as she and Sheila sat on the floor of Sheila's flat, with newspapers spread all around them, 'I've been so busy writing this new play and with all the fuss and excitement, I've never given a thought to poor Ailsa.'

'Let's drive up to Drim this weekend,' said

Sheila. 'I'd like to see Hamish Macbeth again. That poor man. The number of times I stood him up. I'll phone him.'

'Tell him not to tell anyone we're coming,' said Eileen.

'Are you worried about Colin?'

'Not any more. But I'd like to make our arrival in Drim a surprise.'

Sheila phoned Hamish. 'I feel the least I can do is buy you a meal,' she said. 'If you're fed up with me, I quite understand.'

'No,' said Hamish. 'But turn up this time. When?'

'We're driving up on Saturday. Saturday evening at the Napoli at eight?'

'That'll be grand. How does it feel to be successful?'

'Great.'

'Harry Frame must be furious with you.'

'He tried to offer me a job. Can you believe it? I had great pleasure in telling him to get lost. See you Saturday. Oh, and we want to surprise them in Drim, so don't tell anyone.'


It was odd to be approaching Drim again, thought Eileen, blinking out at familiar landmarks through her new contact lenses. Sheila drove down the winding road that led down to Drim, then parked outside the general stores.

'Well, here we are,' said Sheila as she and Eileen stepped out of the car.

'This looks like a welcoming committee,' laughed Eileen. The women of Drim were coming down from their cottages towards them. Ailsa came out of the shop and stood with her arms folded, her face grim.

'Ailsa!' cried Eileen, making to run towards her.

'Keep your distance,' shouted Ailsa.

'There's something badly wrong here,' said Sheila nervously, watching the women get closer.

Then Holly Andrews, who was at the head of the group, stood and yanked up a clod of grass and earth and hurled it straight at them.

'Bitch!' shouted Holly. 'You made money out o' us! Bitch!'

A wind raced down the loch, whipping Eileen's skirts about her legs. Crows dived and screamed overhead.

'Get in the car,' shouted Sheila, her face white.

They drove off as stones rattled against the sides of the car.

'Where to?' panted Eileen.

'Back to Glasgow,' said Sheila. 'I'm never coming here again.'


Willie Lamont leaned against Hamish's table in the restaurant that evening and said, 'Stood up again?'

'It looks like that,' said Hamish gloomily.

'It's your reputation for philately that puts the women off.'

'I suppose you mean philandering, Willie. Who am I supposed to be philandering with? You?'

'No need to get so shirty,' said Willie, backing off.

This is my life, thought Hamish, sitting in a restaurant waiting for some woman who can't even be bothered to turn up.

Jimmy Anderson walked in.

'I've been looking for you,' he said. 'Patricia Martyn-Broyd's just topped herself.'

'How did she do it?'

'Hanged herself on a bit o' sheet. Well, less money for the taxpayer to bother about. You on your own, Hamish?'

'Yes.'

'Good, I'm right hungry. There's nothing like a plate o' spaghetti washed down wi' a glass o' Scotch.'

Jimmy sat down and shook out his napkin. 'Sure you weren't waiting for anyone, were you?'

'As a matter of fact, I've been stood up.'

'That's the women for ye,' said Jimmy. 'And do ye know the answer, Hamish?'

'No.'

'Get drunk!'

If you enjoyed *Death of a Scriptwriter*, read on for the first chapter of the next book in the *Hamish Macbeth* series . . .

# DEATH
## of an ADDICT

# Chapter One

*Shall man into the mystery of breath*
*From his quick breathing pulse a pathway spy?*
*Or learn the secret of the shrouded death.*
*By lifting up the lid of a white eye?*
                              – George Meredith

Hamish Macbeth drove along a rutted single-track road on a fine September day. The mountains of Sutherland soared up to a pale blue sky. There had been weeks of heavy rain and everything seemed scrubbed clean and the air was heavy with the smell of pine and wild thyme.

It was a good day to be alive. In fact, for one lanky red-haired Highland policeman who had just discovered he was heart-whole again, it was heaven.

The once love of his life, Priscilla Halburton-Smythe, had been home to the Highlands on a brief visit. They had gone out for dinner together and his mind had probed his treacherous heart but had found nothing stronger lurking in there but simple liking.

The sun was shining and somewhere out there were charming girls, beautiful girls, girls who would be only too happy to give their love and their lives to one Hamish Macbeth.

The vast heathery area of his beat which lay outside the village of Lochdubh had been crime-free, and so he had little to do but look after his small croft at the back of the police station, feed his sheep and hens, mooch around in his lazy way and dream of nothing in particular.

His beat had of late merely been a series of social calls – a cup of tea at some farm, a cup of coffee in some whitewashed little croft house. He was on his way to visit a crofter called Parry McSporran, who lived up in the wilderness of moorland near the source of the River Anstey, just outside the village of Glenanstey.

There are two types of Highlander, the entrepreneur and the cowboy. The entrepreneurs are hardworking, and set up schemes to earn money from tourists, and the cowboys are usually drunken louts, jealous of the entrepreneurs, and set out to sabotage their efforts. A taxi driver, for instance, who started to build up a successful business would suddenly find he was getting calls to pick up people in remote places and when he got there, he would find the call had been a hoax. One who had started a trout farm found the water had been poisoned.

Parry McSporran had built three small holiday chalets on his land. During the building of them, he had experienced some trouble. Building materials had mysteriously gone missing; rude spray-painted graffiti desecrated his house walls.

Hamish had tracked down the youths who had done the damage and had threatened them with prison. After that Parry had been left in peace. He had recently started to take in long lets. He said this way he saved himself the bother of changing linen every week and cleaning the chalets. It was a good move, for the tourist season in Sutherland, that county which is as far north in mainland Britain as you can go, was very short.

Parry was moving his sheep from one field to the other when Hamish arrived. He waved. Hamish waved back and leaned against the fence to watch Parry's sheepdogs at work. There was nothing better, he reflected lazily, than watching a couple of excellent sheepdogs at work on this perfect day. All it would take to complete the bliss would be a cigarette. Stop that, he told his brain severely. He had given up smoking some time ago, but occasionally the craving for one would come unbidden, out of nowhere.

The transfer of the sheep being completed, Parry waved Hamish towards the croft house.

'Come ben,' he said. 'You are chust in time for the cup of tea.'

'Grand,' said Hamish, following him into the stone-flagged kitchen. Parry was not married. According to all reports, he had never wanted to get married. He was a small, wiry man with sandy hair and an elfin face with those light grey eyes which give little away, as if their bright intelligence masked any feeling lurking behind them in the same way that a man walking into a dim room after bright sunlight will not be able to distinguish the objects lying around.

'Got anyone for your chalets?' asked Hamish, sitting down at the kitchen table.

'I haff the two long lets,' said Parry, 'and the other one is booked up by families for the summer.'

'Who are your long lets?' asked Hamish as Parry lifted the kettle off the black top of the Raeburn stove which he kept burning, winter and summer.

'In number one is Felicity Maundy, English, Green.'

'You mean she's a virgin?'

'Come on, Hamish. Don't be daft. I mean one o' thae save-the-world Greens. She is worried about the global warmings.'

'In the Highlands!' exclaimed Hamish. 'A wee bit o' the global warming up here would chust be grand.'

'Aye, but she chust shakes her heid and says it's coming one day.'

He put a mug of tea in front of Hamish. 'Pretty?' asked Hamish.

'If you like that sort of thing.'

'What sort of thing?'

'Wispy hair, wispy clothes, big boots, no make-up.'

'And what is she doing up here in Glenanstey?' asked Hamish curiously.

'Herself is finding the quality of life.'

'Oh, one of those.'

'Aye, but she's been here three months now and seems happy enough. Writes poems.'

Hamish lost interest in Felicity. 'What about the other one?'

'Nice young man. Tommy Jarret. Early twenties. Writing a book.'

'Oh, aye,' said Hamish cynically. The ones who locked themselves away from civilization to write a book were usually the ones who couldn't write anywhere. 'Jarret,' he mused. 'That rings a bell.'

'Meaning he has a criminal record?'

'Probably not, Parry. I'll check into it if you like.'

'Aye, do that. I'd be grateful to ye, Hamish.'

'Mr McSporran,' called a soft voice from the open doorway. 'I wondered if I could buy some eggs from you.'

Hamish swung round. This, then, must be Felicity Maundy. The sunlight streaming in through the kitchen door shone through her thin Indian-style dress of fine patterned cotton and turned the wisps of her no-colour hair into an aureole. She moved forward into the shadow revealing herself to be a thin, young girl with a pale anxious face and nervous pale blue eyes which slid this way and that.

She was wearing a heavy string of amber beads which made her neck look fragile. Under the long skirts of her dress, she was wearing a pair of what looked like army boots.

'I'll get some for ye,' said Parry. 'Sit down. This here is Hamish Macbeth.'

Felicity nervously eyed Hamish's uniform. 'I'll just stand.' Her voice was as soft and insubstantial as her appearance.

'How do you pass the time up here, Miss Maundy?' asked Hamish.

'What do you mean?' There was now a shrill edge to her voice.

'I mean,' said Hamish patiently, 'it's a wee bit remote here. Don't you find it lonely?'

'Oh, not at all!' She spread her arms in a theatrical gesture. 'The hills and the birds are my companions.'

'Och,' snorted Parry, returning with a box of eggs, 'you should put on some make-up and heels and go down to Strathbane and have some fun.'

'I do not wear make-up,' said Felicity primly.

'Why not?' asked Parry. 'You could do with a wee bit o' colour in your face.'

'If one wears make-up,' declaimed Felicity as if reciting a well-rehearsed line, 'people cannot see the real you.'

'I shouldn't think anyone could see you, real or otherwise, hidden out here,' remarked Hamish.

Felicity ignored him.

'How much do I owe you for the eggs?'

'No charge today.'

'Oh, thank you. You are just too, too kind.'

Felicity whipped up the box and disappeared out of the kitchen door.

'That one's got you for a sucker,' remarked Hamish.

'Aw, she's chust the wee bit o' a thing. Needs building up. Will you check up on Tommy Jarret for me, Hamish?'

'I'll do it now,' said Hamish. 'Won't be a minute. I've got a phone in the car, although thae mobiles can be a pain. The number of places in the Highlands where they won't work!'

He went out to the police Land Rover and picked up his mobile phone and dialled police headquarters in Strathbane and got through to Jenny McSween, nicknamed the Keeper of the Records.

'Wait a minute, Hamish,' said Jenny. 'I'll just feed that name into the computer.'

Hamish leaned against the side of the Land Rover and waited, enjoying the feel of the sun on his face. The three holiday chalets were hidden behind screens of birch trees to give the occupants privacy. Through the flickering leaves of birch he could see Felicity's pale face at a window.

Then Jenny's voice came on the phone. 'Thomas Jarret, arrested last year, for possession of ecstasy and cannabis. Got off a pushing charge. Said they were for his own use and since only small amounts were found, he got away with it. Arresting detective, Jimmy Anderson, thinks he was pushing but couldn't make anything stick. Thomas Jarret was or is a heroin addict, you see.'

'I see,' said Hamish bleakly. 'Thanks, Jenny.'

He went back into the croft house and told Parry what he had learned.

'I'll haff that cheil out on his ear,' growled Parry. 'I cannae thole drugs.'

'Let's go and have a word with him,' said Hamish. 'He may be reformed. I'm all for giving folks a break.'

Parry, his face grim, walked ahead of Hamish and towards one of the chalets. He knocked at the door. 'Mr Jarret, we'll chust be having a wee word wi' ye.'

The door opened and a pleasant-looking young man stood there. He had a mop of curly brown hair and brown eyes in a tanned face. Those blinked rapidly when he saw Hamish's uniform.

'Can we come in?' asked Hamish.

'Y-yes.'

He backed away into the chalet living room. A word processor was on a table by the window, surrounded with piles of manuscript.

'Sit down,' said Tommy nervously.

'I'll get straight to the point,' said Hamish, sitting down and taking off his peaked cap and then twisting it round and round in his hands. 'You were arrested for possession of drugs. The arresting detective was convinced you were pushing.'

'I've been clean for six months. Honest,' pleaded Tommy. 'And I wasn't pushing. I went to a rehab in Strathbane. Ask anyone. In fact, I'm writing a book about my experience with drugs to warn other people what it's like.'

'Why were you found in possession of ecstasy and cannabis when you were a heroin addict?' asked Hamish.

Tommy gave a rueful smile. 'If you can't get your drug of choice, you'll go for anything.' He rolled up his shirtsleeves. 'Look, no track marks, and Mr McSporran here will tell you he's never seen me other than sober.'

'It iss not the drink I'm worried about,' said Parry.

'It's therapy-speak,' explained Hamish. 'Sober means he hasn't taken any mood-altering chemical. Am I right, Tommy?'

'Yes, I never even drink booze now. Please give me a chance,' said Tommy earnestly. 'You know I haven't been any trouble, Mr McSporran, and I pay my rent on time.'

'Aye, that's right,' said Parry reluctantly.

Hamish made up his mind. 'I'd let him be for the moment, Parry. I believe what he says.'

Outside in the sunlight, Parry said, 'You seem mighty sure of yourself, Hamish.'

'Like I said, I'm all for giving folks a chance. He seems a nice fellow to me. Come on, Parry. Strathbane's become a sink o' iniquity. I've seen a lot of good young people wrecked. This one seems to have pulled himself together.'

'I s'pose,' said Parry. 'He's no trouble. Let's hope your judgement is right, Hamish Macbeth.'

'Och, I am never wrong,' said Hamish with simple Highland vanity.

But when he had returned to Lochdubh and locked his hens away for the night, Hamish went into the police station office and phoned Detective Jimmy Anderson.

'Tommy Jarret?' said Jimmy in answer to Hamish's query. 'I mind him. Got away with possession and up in front of a lenient sheriff. Got nothing more than a stay in a rehab and a hundred days' community service.'

'Wait a bit,' said Hamish. 'He was a heroin addict?'

'Aye.'

'That's a pretty expensive drug to be taking

in the Highlands of Scotland. Where did he get the money?'

'Some aunt of his left him money, seems to be true. Respectable parents. Well off. Father a bank manager. Neat bungalow outside Strathbane, member of the Rotary Club, polishes the car on Sunday, get the picture? So he can afford heroin. I tell you another thing that made me mad. Couldn't get out of him where he got his supply from. I mean, he's lucky to be alive.'

'Why's that?'

'I believe there's a lot of adulterated stuff around and some bastard at the Three Bells pub down at the old docks was pushing talcum powder. The street price of heroin in Aberdeen was a hundred pounds per gram. Why are you asking about Tommy Jarret?'

'The name cropped up,' said Hamish.

'Meaning the wee bastard's in your parish. I don't trust any o' thae junkies.'

'Lot of drugs in Strathbane?' asked Hamish.

'Aye, it's a plague. It's the new motorways. We're no longer cut off up here so they zoom up the motorways from Glasgow and Manchester. The drug barons make money and more young people die every year.'

'What would happen, I wonder,' mused Hamish, 'if the stuff were legalized? I mean, there would be controls on the quality of the stuff and all the drug barons and drug cartels would be out of business.'

'Whit! It's statements like that which explain why you're a copper and I'm a detective. That's a load of dangerous rubbish you're talking, Hamish.'

'Just thought I would ask,' said Hamish meekly.

He rang off and then changed into his civilian clothes and went out for a stroll along the waterfront. He didn't mind at all being a mere village copper. Hamish Macbeth had side-stepped promotion to Strathbane several times. The waters of Lochdubh lay placid under a pale sky, with only the ripples from a porpoise to disturb the calm surface. The violent world of cities such as Strathbane seemed pleasingly remote.

'Dreaming, Hamish?'

Hamish, who had been leaning against the harbour wall, turned and found Dr Brodie's wife, Angela, surveying him with amusement.

'I was thinking of pretty much nothing,' said Hamish. 'Except maybe drugs.'

'I don't think we've got any cases in Lochdubh.'

'Good.'

She leaned against the harbour wall beside him and he turned back and rested his arms against the rough stone, still warm from the day's sunshine.

'Why do people take drugs, Angela?'

'Because they like the effect. You should

know a simple thing like that, Hamish. Then in the young, it's bad and exciting.'

'But all those warnings,' protested Hamish. 'All those kids dying from ecstasy pills.'

'Addicts never think it'll happen to them. And the young feel immortal anyway.'

'What if it were legalized?'

'I don't know. I don't think so. The illegality itself is a deterrent. Can you imagine if young people, children maybe, had unlimited access to LSD?'

'You're right,' said Hamish with a sigh. 'What's the solution?'

'Everyone starts refusing?'

'I cannae envisage that.'

'It could happen. Just become unfashionable. Like smoking. You're having a quiet time these days, Hamish.'

'Long may it last. I wouldnae like to see another murder in Lochdubh.'

'There may be one shortly.'

'Who? What?'

'Nessie and Jessie Currie are joint chairwomen of the Mothers' Union at the church this year.'

'Oh, dear.' Jessie and Nessie were middle-aged twin sisters, both unmarried.

'The others are complaining it's like being run by the Gestapo.'

'Can't they vote them out?'

'Not for another year.'

'What are they doing that's so bad?'

'Well, at the cake sale, they criticized the quality of the baking and reduced little Mrs McWhirter to tears, for one. Then they have lately become obsessed with germs and the church hall has to be regularly scrubbed. They have pinned up a cleaning rota and all women must remove their shoes before entering the hall.'

'I'll have a word with them.'

'Would you, Hamish? I don't know what you can say. Everyone's tried.'

'I'll have a go.'

Hamish said goodbye to her and strolled off in the direction of the Currie sisters' cottage.

He knocked at the highly polished brass lion's head on the door. Jessie answered, blinking up at him through her thick glasses. 'It's you. It's you,' said Jessie, who had an irritating way of repeating everything.

'I just dropped by for a wee word,' said Hamish easily.

'Come ben.' Hamish ducked his head and followed Jessie into the living room, where sister Nessie was seated.

Nessie was knitting ferociously, steel pins flashing through magenta wool.

'What brings you?' asked Nessie.

Hamish sat down. 'I'll get tea. I'll get tea,' said Jessie.

Hamish raised a hand. 'Not for me, thank you. This'll only take a minute.'

Jessie folded her arms and eyed the tall

red-haired policeman nervously. 'It must be serious for you to refuse a free cup of tea, free cup of tea.'

'It iss the little matter o' the Mothers' Union.'

Nessie stopped knitting. 'What's up wi' the Mothers' Union?'

'The pair of you are what's up with it.'

'What d'ye mean, d'ye mean?' demanded Jessie. 'We run it wi' an iron hand, iron hand.'

'Well, now, ladies, the iron hand seems to be the trouble. Ye cannae go on like the Gestapo.'

'Who's complaining?' demanded Nessie wrathfully.

'Chust about everyone,' said Hamish Macbeth.

'We've done nothing wrong, nothing wrong,' said Jessie. 'We've made sure the church hall is clean, and that place was a sewer, a sewer.'

'Yes, and it iss the grand job the pair of you are doing at fighting the germs, but is there any need to fight the others?' Hamish reflected it was an odd world when the Mothers' Union was being run by two childless spinsters. Did anyone ever use the word 'spinster' any more? What was politically correct? 'Miz' was irritating and pretentious. Single? And why should women who were not married be considered strange in any way? He was not married himself.

'I'm speaking to you, Hamish Macbeth,' shouted Nessie, penetrating his thoughts, 'and all you can do is sit there like a gormless loon after insulting us.'

'Insulting us,' chorused Jessie.

'I wass thinking about Margaret Thatcher,' lied Hamish.

'What about her?' asked Nessie, a look of reverence in her eyes.

The sisters adored Margaret Thatcher.

'Well, now, Mrs Thatcher –'

'*Baroness* Thatcher,' corrected the Currie sisters in unison.

'Lady Thatcher, then. Now, herself would run that Mothers' Union with a firm hand. But she would delegate responsibility, draw everyone in. You get more out of people if they like you. Diplomacy is the word, ladies.'

'And what do you know about Lady Thatcher?' jeered Nessie.

Hamish half-closed his eyes. 'It wass the great day,' he crooned, his Highland accent becoming more sibilant as he worked himself up to telling one massive lie. 'I wass down in Inverness and there she wass, just doing her shopping like you or me.'

'When was this, when was this?' cried Jessie.

'Let me see, it would be June last year, a fine day, I 'member.'

'What was she buying?' asked Nessie, her eyes shining.

'It was in Marks and Spencer. She wass looking at one of thae tailored blouses she likes to wear. Silk, it was.'

'And did you speak to her?'

'I did that,' said Hamish.

'What did you say?'

'I asked her to autograph my notebook, which she did. I asked her the secret of success.'

Both sisters leaned forward. 'And she said?'

'She said the secret was the firm hand.'

'Ah!'

'But with kindness, she said. She wass as near to me as you are now. She said she never let herself get bogged down wi' bullying people or bothering about the small stuff. "If you work hard," she says to me, "you do the service for others chust because you want to. The minute you start pushing people and bragging about how hard you are working for them, they turn against you. Nobody wants a martyr."'

The sisters looked at each other. 'Maybe we have been a bit too strong, bit too strong,' said Jessie.

'Aye, maybe we'll go a bit easier,' said Nessie. 'And then what did she say?'

'Dennis, her husband, came up at that minute and he says, "You're neffer going to buy that blouse, Maggie. The colour's wrong." It wass the purple silk.'

'I'll bet she told him to take a running jump,' said Nessie.

'Not herself. She chust smiled and said, "Yes, dear, you're probably right." You see there

293

wass the security men all about her and a lady like that wasn't going to stoop to be petty.'

'What a woman, what a woman,' breathed Jessie. 'We shall neffer see her like again.'

Hamish stood up, his red head almost brushing the low ceiling. 'I'll be on my way, ladies.'

'Can we see that autograph, Hamish?'

'Och, no, I sent it to my cousin Rory in New Hampshire. He has it framed and hung over his fireplace.'

Hamish made his way out. In the small hallway was a framed photograph of Margaret Thatcher. He winked at it and let himself out.

He ambled back towards the police station. As he approached Patel's, the general store, he recognized the waiflike figure of Felicity Maundy. In the same moment, she saw him and her face turned a muddy colour. She unlocked the door of an old Metro, threw her groceries on to the passenger seat, climbed in and drove off leaving a belch of exhaust hanging in the air.

'Now, what's she got on her conscience?' murmured Hamish. 'Probably went on some demo when she was a wee lassie at school and thinks the police still have a eye on her.'

He shrugged and proceeded along to the police station. His rambling roses at the front were still doing well and their blossoms almost hid the blue police lamp.

Hamish began to plan a relaxed evening,

maybe put on a casserole and let it simmer and go to the pub for an hour. The new alcopops had turned out to be a menace, those sweet fizzy alcoholic drinks. They had been designed, in his opinion, to seduce the young, but it was the Highlanders, the fishermen in particular, every man of them having a sweet tooth, who had become hooked on them. So Hamish meant to combine pleasure and duty by keeping a sharp eye on the drivers who were drinking over the limit. Then he would return at closing time and start taking away car keys.

He opened the kitchen door and went in. The phone in the police station office began to ring shrilly. He went quickly to answer it. He experienced a blank feeling of dread and tried to shrug it off. It would be nothing more than a minor complaint. Or a hoax call.

He picked up the receiver. 'Lochdubh police,' he said.

'Hamish, this is Parry. It's yon fellow, Tommy Jarret. He's dead.'

'Dead. How? Why?'

'They think it's an overdose. They found a syringe.'

'I'll be right over.'

Cursing, Hamish rapidly changed into his uniform. How could it all have happened so quickly? he thought. The lad had been all right. What had happened to his, Hamish Macbeth's, famous intuition? He could have sworn Tommy Jarret was not in danger of returning to his drug taking.

He drove off up the winding road leading out of Lochdubh towards Glenanstey, his heart heavy. Large black clouds were building up behind the mountains. They seemed like black omens, harbingers of trouble to come.

**To order your copies** of other books in the Hamish Macbeth series simply contact The Book Service (TBS) by phone, email or by post. Alternatively visit our website at www.constablerobinson.com.

| No. of copies | Title | RRP | Total |
|---|---|---|---|
| | Death of a Gossip | £6.99 | |
| | Death of a Cad | £6.99 | |
| | Death of an Outsider | £6.99 | |
| | Death of a Perfect Wife | £6.99 | |
| | Death of a Hussy | £6.99 | |
| | Death of a Snob | £6.99 | |
| | Death of a Prankster | £6.99 | |
| | Death of a Glutton | £6.99 | |
| | Death of a Travelling Man | £6.99 | |
| | Death of a Charming Man | £6.99 | |
| | Death of a Nag | £6.99 | |
| | Death of a Macho Man | £6.99 | |
| | Death of a Dentist | £6.99 | |
| | Death of a Scriptwriter | £6.99 | |
| | Death of an Addict | £6.99 | |
| | A Highland Christmas | £5.99 | |
| | Death of a Dustman | £6.99 | |
| | Death of a Celebrity | £6.99 | |
| | Death of a Village | £6.99 | |
| | Death of a Poison Pen | £6.99 | |
| | Death of a Bore | £6.99 | |
| | Death of a Dreamer | £6.99 | |
| | Death of a Maid | £6.99 | |
| | Death of a Gentle Lady | £6.99 | |
| | Death of a Witch | £6.99 | |
| | Death of a Valentine | £6.99 | |
| | Death of a Sweep (hardback) | £18.99 | |
| Grand total | | | £ |

FREEPOST RLUL-SJGC-SGKJ, Cash Sales Direct Mail Dept., The Book Service, Colchester Road, Frating, Colchester, CO7 7DW. Tel: +44 (0) 1206 255 800.
Fax: +44 (0) 1206 255 930. Email: sales@tbs-ltd.co.uk

UK customers: please allow £1.00 p&p for the first book, plus 50p for the second, and an additional 30p for each book thereafter, up to a maximum charge of £3.00. Overseas customers (incl. Ireland): please allow £2.00 p&p for the first book, plus £1.00 for the second, plus 50p for each additional book.

NAME (block letters): _____

ADDRESS: _____

_____

_____ POSTCODE: _____

I enclose a cheque/PO (payable to 'TBS Direct') for the amount

of £_____

I wish to pay by Switch/Credit Card

Card number: _____

Expiry date: _____ Switch issue number: _____